Three Hearts In Love

Cascade Bay, Volume 4

Solara Gordon

Published by THE EARTH MOVED, LLC, 2023.

THREE HEARTS IN LOVE

First edition. June 19, 2023.

Copyright © 2023 Solara Gordon.

ISBN: 979-8986032597

Written by Solara Gordon.

Also by Solara Gordon

Cascade Bay
Love Reborn
Reunited By Choice
Love's Triple Play
Three Hearts In Love

Cauldron Falls
Believe In Love
A Christmas Reunion

Peyton Corners
Falling for You
Caught by Love's Slow Burn

Standalone
A Heart's Desire
To Love You Again
To Love You Again

Watch for more at https://solaragordon.com/.

This one is for the readers, the dreamers and creatives, the people who dare to live and love differently. This is for the polyamory folks who are out there living and loving honesty and openly. Here's to my readers group, Solara's Glamourous Stars, thank you for your support and inspiration!!

Smiles,

Solara Gordon

Chapter One

"*Janet, you set me up?*" Tina Davidson winced at the harshness of her voice as she watched her best friend finish applying her makeup. "A costume party doesn't require a date."

Janet Morton smiled as she picked up her costume and moved into the guest bathroom, leaving the door ajar as their conversation continued. "The invitation said gender balanced. If I hadn't set you up, Rodger would have had to turn you away. You know what sticklers his parents are."

Tina tossed her brush into her tote bag, wondering how long she could keep her frustration in check. Her experience with blind dates racked up a high score in undesirable and never again. As Janet's maid of honor, she couldn't back out.

Combing her fingers through her shoulder-length auburn hair, Tina separated the strands into three bunches and began braiding. "I refuse to lose my cool over this."

Janet's laughter bubbled out the door. "Practicing your sixties-speak? I'm sorry I didn't tell you sooner."

"Right, and Hades has ice forming as we speak." Tina wrapped a bright, tie-dyed ribbon around the end of her braid. The ribbon matched the t-shirt and mini-skirt she wore. She tightly secured the ribbon's ends and shook her head, which eased her hair off her shoulder and out of her way. She added jewelry and earrings as her last items. "Tell me about my date."

"You met Drake and Jon shortly after Rodger and I started dating. It's not like they're strangers. Rodger doesn't know who chose you or Nita."

No matter how reassuring Janet tried to sound, Tina wasn't comforted. Yes, she'd met them briefly over the first year Rodger and Janet dated. That didn't mean Jon or Drake was attracted to her.

Tina eyed the mirror one last time, wishing she'd remembered to pack her contacts. Her dark frames stood out in contrast to the bright colors she wore. At least there was no mistaking her blue eyes. They shone clearly whether she wore contacts or glasses. A grin came and went as a line from her high school days flashed through her mind. She wasn't wearing birth control glasses. Those days were long gone.

Janet stepped out of the bathroom. Her vintage roaring twenties flapper dress came to her knees. Thin spaghetti straps sparkled against her lightly tanned shoulders. The deep mauve color offset by light pink lace and glass bead accents complemented her. The dress hugged her curves in places Tina wished hers didn't accent her full-figure curves. Envy wasn't a feeling Tina even considered as Janet turned around in front of the mirror.

"I'm glad I stopped being jealous of you a long time ago." Tina smiled as Janet slipped her shoes on. "That color is perfect for you. I hope Rodger realizes this."

Janet smiled as she bent to buckle her baby-doll heels. "I'm sure he'll notice. His mother hasn't seen the outfit. She fussed about approving everyone's costumes."

"I bet Rodger rolled his eyes and counted to a hundred more than once." Tina pulled on her knee-high boots, zipped them up, and stood.

"He spent the last two weeks with me. To quote him, 'Mother needs to let go 'cuz the apron strings are long gone.'" Janet grabbed her tote and purse. "Shall we go meet my in-laws-to-be?"

Tina sighed, stuffed the rest of her belongings into her tote, and slung her purse over her shoulder. "What a way to meet Rodger's relatives and the rest of the wedding party."

Janet nodded. "Can't say it isn't unique. A costume party for the bride and groom."

Tina snorted as she caught Janet's saucy wink and exaggerated wiggle as she walked away from her. Janet still hadn't said one thing about if it was Drake or Jon waiting with Rodger as her date.

Two floors below them, Rodger Daniels tugged at the collar of his tuxedo. Out of the corner of his eye, he could see his mother fervently shaking her head. When would the woman realize he'd grown up? His sister stood beside her so ramrod stiff, he'd swear she had a pole up her . . .

"Haven't you learned to ignore your mom yet?" Jon Smithson chuckled as he stepped up beside Rodger. "She's going to keep on until you tell her off."

"Right, and then Aunt Helen is going to be complaining more." Drake Cranston rose from where he sat. "Now which side am I supposed to wear the patch on?"

Rodger glanced from Jon to Drake. Both wore pirate outfits with eye patches and almost identical colored shirts. Why couldn't Janet let one of them be Tina's date? No, she asked both before she heard back from either of them. With one bridesmaid out due to illness, two pirates awaited Tina.

"I don't know what Janet told you." Rodger shrugged and undid his bowtie. To hell with what his mother said or did. Dressing up like the help and letting the help dress up like them was madness. Twice he'd been asked for more champagne. Hell, they hadn't opened it yet. A whiskey neat and straight up was more what he had in mind.

"I could use a drink. What about you?" Rodger walked away, leaving Jon and Drake where they stood.

Jon held up his eye patch. "Are you going to put yours on?"

"We've got to. I think Janet told me left eye. So yours would be right?" Drake pulled his eye patch out of his waist pack.

"How about we forgo them instead?" Jon offered, stretching the elastic band on his between his hands. "How are we supposed to see with them on?"

Drake snickered and grinned. "Out of the eye that isn't covered."

"Smart mouth, I know that. I'm talking about the one that's covered. There's a peephole in the patch." Jon held his patch up, squinting as he moved it around and closer to him.

"A what?" Drake arched his eyebrow. He glanced toward the bar where Rodger stood, sipping his drink.

"A peephole. You know, a place you can see through so you don't bump into things." Jon's infectious grin had Drake catching his tongue between his teeth to keep from laughing.

"Mine has a mesh piece that allows me to see through it." Drake tossed his patch at Jon. "Do we need them since we're escorting Tina?"

Jon caught the patch, gave it the once over, and stuffed it in his hand with his. "At least we didn't get stuck with the outrageous feathered hat!"

Drake rolled his eyes and held out his hand. "Give me those things before you decide to revert to your youth."

Jon shook his head as he handed the patches to him. "Like I am going to attempt to shoot anything with those things."

Drake put the patches into his waist pack and zipped it closed. "Aunt Helen still talks about your slingshot incident with shooting the rotten tomatoes into the fireplace."

"I've grown up. Aunt Helen still mothers us and smothers Rodger." Jon placed his tricorn hat on his head and moved toward the buffet.

"Let's see if we can find our date." Drake put on a similar hat and followed in Jon's wake.

Janet stashed Tina's tote with hers in the closet in her room. "I don't know why you can't stay here for the weekend. You knew about this before Frank weaseled you into taking the extra shift."

"Like I could turn down the extra money. Time and a half will help cushion my savings account and replenish the pantry." Tina fastened a thin belt around her waist, threading it through the strap of the small leather clutch she'd stashed her cash and ID in.

"Yes, I get it. I can't fault you." Janet tugged her beaded headband over her head. "I hope you land a great job once you graduate."

Janet slid her arm around Tina's waist. Tina leaned into the hug she knew was coming. Her bestie understood her. She hoped Rodger knew what a prize he was getting. He probably did. He'd proposed six months after he and Janet began dating. Tina smiled as Janet released her and stepped back.

"I've got two more classes. Come fall, I'm a certified life coach. Working for Frank will be passé." Janet returned her smile. Tina hadn't added that two of her recent interviews looked promising. Getting back to them topped her list of priorities once the weekend ended.

Janet started out of the guest bedroom ahead of Tina. She stopped as she entered the hall. "Wish both of us good luck. Me with Rodger's relatives and you with ditching Frank."

Tina eased her way past Janet. "Come on, woman. Nothing and no one can daunt us tonight." Tina strode down the hall, glancing over her shoulder, making sure Janet kept up with her.

As they reached the top of the stairs, music and the sound of chatter greeted them. Tina sucked in air as she counted twenty people near the stairs alone. How many people had Rodger's mother invited? Raising her gaze, she counted twice as many standing near the bar and buffet area. Great, a huge gathering that rivaled the number of guests at most weddings she had attended. So much for the intimate group get-together Janet had asked for. With formal invitations, what had either of them expected?

Janet gripped Tina's hand as she leaned close, whispering, "Shit, my future mother-in-law invited everyone she could. Possibly the ones Rodger and I crossed off the guest list."

Tina rubbed her lips together, hoping she didn't start giggling. Nerves aside, Rodger's grandmother was worse than his mother and sister combined. Old money didn't take well to new, younger, medium-income folks marrying into their families. Rodger didn't care. He'd made his own way without his family helping. With a successful architecture business built and new contracts flowing in, he didn't have to worry. Neither did Janet. Her business had increased twice in the past six months. Interior decorating and design partnered with architecture amazingly well.

"Do I tell them off for you or . . ." Tina caught the glow in Janet's eye right before she winked. Tina bet Janet's wicked wit simmered next to her frustration and irritation. By evening's end, they'd have to compare notes to see who succeeded in telling someone off nicely and the person not noticing it.

As Janet moved down the stairs, Tina noted the subtle changes in her posture and speech. Gone was the easygoing woman she knew and loved. A protective facade formed around her molding to show a polite, successful businesswoman. Tina wondered how long this would hold up.

Toward the bottom of the staircase, two men stood dressed in similar costumes. Drake, with short-cropped brown hair, and Jon, who wore his blond hair a bit longer. They appeared equal in stature. Tina swallowed hard. She could gaze at either man for several moments while her mind raced through several fantasies. Closing her eyes briefly, she waited as she inhaled deeply. One last look wouldn't hurt. She blinked, glanced at the two, and followed Janet the rest of the way down the stairs.

Rodger looked away from where his mother stood in front of him, mouthing another item she felt important. His one drink had turned into two.

The second sat unfinished on the bar. The woman's voice reminded him of fingernails grating down a chalkboard. His grandmother stood rigidly straight behind his mother, glaring at him as she squinted behind her thick lenses and silver frames. Her bluish-tinted hair almost matched her dress. Rodger bit the inside of his lip to keep from telling her what he thought of her prudish look and face. Where the hell was Janet? Mother wouldn't open the buffet and seat people until Janet and her maid of honor entered. One more damn lap through the maze and he'd forget manners. Jumping over the tables and overturning the chairs to make his getaway good tempted him greatly. Damn good thing the room was as large as it was given all the people Mother invited. Who knew they could fit a double U formation in there with twenty-five tables?

A loud knock echoed throughout the large formal dining room. Their butler stood between two women. All eyes were probably on them. One more of Mother's formalities, everyone was announced as they entered the festivities.

"Ladies and gentlemen, I present the bride, Ms. Janet Morton, and her matron of honor, Ms. Tina Davidson."

Rodger elbowed his mother aside, mumbling an apology. His father nodded as he passed him. The old man understood. He'd keep the old bats in check while Rodger claimed his bride-to-be.

Chapter Two

Janet held out her hand as Rodger approached. She'd seen the look on his face as she made her way down the stairs. His mother stood in front of him with her mouth moving rapidly. His father stood behind her. Off to Rodger's other side, his grandmother's stiff posture left nothing to guess at. Poor Rodger. Janet bet both women would give him a piece of their minds later.

"Hi, love," Rodger said. His voice took on the low tone that wrapped around her like he did when they lay in the bathtub together with him deep inside her. Memories flooded her as if they were there with his one hand cupping her breast as he thumbed her nipple and his other between her legs, stroking her throbbing, taut clit.

Tina cleared her throat and moved closer to the couple with eyes only for each other. The red flush creeping up Janet's neck and threatening to overtake her cheeks spoke out loud of where her thoughts were. Time to refocus their attention outward. If the look on Rodger's mother's face marching toward them was any indication of the start of the rest of the evening, Tina was ready to grab Janet and Rodger along with Jon and Drake and run far away.

"Oh, hi, Tina," Rodger offered as he slipped his hand into Janet's. "Glad to see you made it."

Tina nodded while she silently mouthed, "Mother," accenting her message with a slight nod of her head in the direction she faced. "I'm happy to be here, Rodger. Thank you for inviting me," she added out loud as she watched Rodger roll his eyes. His quick, quiet "thank you" barely reached her when Helen Daniels screeched Janet's name.

"Janet darling," Helen's loud, high-pitched drone began. Tina clenched her fists, wanting to move two paces back to quiet the ringing starting in her ears. The woman inched closer, reaching for Janet with her arms opening as if she swooped down on her intended prey.

"Rodger," the older woman behind him demanded in an equally irritating pitch. "Introductions, please."

Tina could feel the older woman's gaze rove over her like a drill sergeant inspecting his troops. She knew that look and the fire that burned beneath it wasn't passion or compassion. It smoldered with venom and a sincere dislike for what she saw. Tina had dealt with her kind over the years. Foster care left no secrets unexposed or pasts hidden. Her adoptive parents cured that. She had no reason to be ashamed of who and what she was. A part of her that remained independent and refused to back down when people looked down at her. The years of standing up for herself lingered, etched deep into her psyche. A strong part of her that often colored her outlook and response to people and their actions. Tina met the woman's stare and refused to look away.

Rodger's wordless sigh moved over Janet and her as if they were all face-to-face. Tina felt for him. He'd alluded to his maternal side of the family more than once as dragonesses from hell. Janet's brief nod pricked Tina's interest. How were they going to do this?

"Janet and Tina, I'd like you to meet my mother and grandmother. Helen Daniels and Sandra Addams." Rodger moved sideways, placing himself not quite between Janet and his mother. Sandra Addams' head bobbed up and down as she gave Janet the same once-over she'd done with Tina. Tina had unclenched her hands several times, willing her composure to remain calm and cool. The old woman appeared to be egging to start a fight. She'd have one if she started things. Tina was ready to give as good as she got.

Tina inhaled, fisted part of her shirt in her hand, and tapped her fingers against her hip as she counted to five twice. Janet could handle herself. Rodger appeared to know what was going on. If they couldn't handle it, well, help was available. Maybe she could convince them to elope tonight.

Janet's hand briefly brushed against her as she moved forward. Warmth flowed over Tina's wrist as Janet stepped in front of her. "Mrs. Daniels, good to see you again. Mrs. Addams, pleasure to meet you."

Tina could only see the side of Janet's face. The smile and tone didn't match. Two against two evened the odds. Tina moved up beside Janet. "Ma'am," she began, facing Rodger's grandmother. "Mrs. Addams, I'm honored to meet you." She offered the woman her hand. Manners and etiquette might get Janet and her through the evening. Tina strengthened her resolve to convince Rodger and Janet to elope.

Sandra Addams barely shook Tina's hand before she dropped it. Tina chewed the inside of her cheek as she turned to face Rodger's mother. The woman had voiced her dislike to Rodger more than once over her. Tina was ready for the woman's phoniness. Lord help her if she laid it on thickly. Tina would call her on it, politely, too, and without preamble.

Helen Daniels extended her hand as Tina faced her. Tina waited all of thirty seconds before firmly grasping the woman's hand and pumping it up and down vigorously. "Pleasure to see you again, Mrs. Daniels. Lovely home. Thank you for inviting me. Too bad I won't be able to enjoy more of your hospitality this weekend."

Tina slowly slid her hand free from Mrs. Daniels's. There was no mistaking the icy, chilled look swiftly crossing the woman's face before her fake smile returned as she faced Rodger and her future daughter-in-law. Tina shuddered as Rodger's sister glared at her before she moved over beside her mother and grandmother. One thing stood out over anything else. Three female dragonesses as in-laws were more than anyone should have to withstand. Definitely, time to convince Rodger and Janet to elope.

"Rodger, I'm famished. Please announce dinner and head up the buffet line." Mrs. Daniel's voice dripped with enough forced niceness to sugar-laden any response Rodger could give. His brief nod and stiffness as he offered Janet his arm made Tina want to chafe hers.

Janet's jaw had to ache from the nonstop smile she'd worn from the moment they'd started down the stairs. Tina inhaled and held her breath while she glanced at the other occupants standing close by. The man with salt-and-pepper hair offered his arm to Mrs. Daniels. Tina couldn't remember Rodger's father's name. He moved as stiffly as Rodger did. There was no mistaking who headed up this family—Mrs. Daniels.

Tina waited as Rodger's cousin and best man, Nathan, stepped up to escort Mrs. Addams. The widow shuffled forward. Tina almost felt sorry for her until she remembered an earlier discussion with Janet. The old woman had practically demanded the pedigree of every person making up the bridal party. Janet had nicely told the old bat, as she called her, that everyone had manners and were productive members of society, a.k.a. had jobs and no criminal arrest records. Tina bit the inside of her cheek again lest she burst out snickering. She bet the old bat would froth at the mouth if she could without making herself look undignified.

The rest of the groomsmen fell into line. Tina looked at Jon and Drake, who held out their arms to her. Both were dressed alike. How had she ended up with two escorts? Wasn't Nita, Janet's college roommate, also supposed to be standing here?

Tina swallowed hard as she moved forward, ready to follow behind Rodger's grandmother.

Both men, dressed as pirates, smiled and winked at her as she moved closer.

Janet had dropped hints about Tina's favorite fantasy over the last few weeks...What had she *done*?

"Allow us, my lady, to escort you to partake in food?" Drake stood a good five inches taller than her. His brown hair curled tightly in places. No wonder he wore it short. Easy to manage, and the way a few curls stood up like miniature horns around his hat gave him an impish quality. Tina glanced to her left.

She had to look up to meet Jon's eyes, too. Deep green with a hint of blue glowed at her as his smile grew. Tina estimated his height to be five foot eight compared to her five-foot-five stature. He wore his blond hair a bit longer than his companion. Jon reminded her of the surfers she sat and watched from her patio apartment near the beach. She swore heat rolled off him as his eyes roved over her. It was as though his thoughts lingered on one thing. His eye-humping caress and the quick pucker of his lips raised her internal temperature more degrees than she could handle. Sweat began pooling along her waist and even in the palms of her hands.

Tina fought hard against the urge to pluck the neck of her shirt to fan herself. She blinked and looked away. No luck in cooling down. Drake stepped closer and his gaze moved over her, scalding many of the same areas Jon's had. Wiping her hands on her skirt, Tina looked straight ahead and began to close the space between her and Rodger's grandmother.

As both men fell in step with her, each tucked one of her hands in the crook of their arm. Heat blasted off them, swarming over her until passion gripped her deep within her. She could almost feel every pulse and beat as want ignited and threatened her composure.

She licked her lips, took a deep breath, and continued to look straight ahead. Rodger's grandmother glared back as though she could read every thought and nuance the men and she silently communicated to each other. The closer they got to the tables, the icier the old woman's glare got.

Partway around the table, Tina noticed Janet and Rodger talking animatedly. She could make out part of what Janet said. Two keywords appeared central to their discussion, "parents" and "family." Tina winced as Janet mouthed two curse words as she glanced over her shoulder. Rodger's mother stood stiffly behind her chair. Her hands almost appeared white-knuckled in her grip of the chair back. Another drink sat on the table near Rodger. His father was nowhere in sight. Great, Rodger was in one of his "I don't give a shit" moods, which left Janet to fend off her future in-laws. Tina knew from Janet's descriptions of past interactions with Mrs. Daniels that the shark was on the prowl, trawling for any bait she could pounce on. Janet needed assistance, and quickly, if dinner wasn't going to erupt into a major battle.

Tina caught her bottom lip between her teeth, breathing deeply as she willed her sense of humor to stop with the ironical quips and scenes flashing through her mind. No food fight from *Animal House* would happen, though that would be a far cry better than a quiet, somber dinner. Separating Janet from Rodger would take a move that wouldn't draw too much attention.

Tina snuck a sideways glance at each of her escorts. A plan formed as they reached their chairs. "Gentlemen, please excuse me while I talk with Janet. I'll be back shortly."

Tina dragged her hands over the muscles on each arm. She felt desire ramp up, demanding a response. She as she dropped her hands in front of her. "Need to rescue Janet."

Jon and Drake stood quietly behind their chairs as if they knew what was happening. Their quirky smiles and nods had Tina wondering if they could read her mind. She couldn't shake the feeling that the three of them would be intimate before the evening was out in ways her mind hadn't even begun to conceive.

Chapter Three

Tina threaded her way through the group of people surrounding Janet and Rodger. She suspected Rodger's shrug and Janet's frown concerned his mother and grandmother. Time for rescue had come.

"Excuse me, Rodger." Tina stuck her arm between Janet and Rodger. "I need to talk to Janet for a moment."

Janet nodded and stepped toward her. Tina moved to her right, putting distance between the dragonesses and them. Any more dirty looks from the dragonesses and keeping her cool would be harder than she imagined. As Janet closed the distance between them, Tina turned her back on the group. She grabbed Janet's hand and tugged hard enough that Janet stumbled a bit. Janet righted herself. "What the hell is your problem?" Janet's sourpuss frown quickly vanished as she looked up. Good heavens, were they watching them that intently?

Tina leaned in so she could whisper without others hearing what she had to say. "Not a damn thing unless you want to keep dealing with Rodger's family on your own. Sit on his side close to me. Five on each side of the table should put a bit of space between us and them. Let him deal with his dragons."

Janet smiled. "Oh, good observation. He's frustrated and working on keeping his tongue in check. I told him more liquor isn't the answer."

"You and I know that. He's tipsy from lack of food. What do you need to do to get things started?"

"Get his mother seated along with everyone else. He keeps saying let his father handle her." Janet scanned the people closest to her. "I guess it's up to me to tell him to do it."

Tina snorted. "Never took Rodger for a submissive. If it works, go for it."

Janet turned and began to walk away. Tina grabbed her wrist and tugged her back. "Whoa, I got a question. What's with me and the two dudes?"

Janet grinned and rolled her eyes heavenward. Tina tightened her grip and sighed. "Tell me," she began, pausing before she ground out the rest of her statement. "Now. *Please.*"

Two escorts for dinner wasn't bad but with the dragonesses and old bat watching practically every move she and Janet made, knowing what was going on made sense.

Janet glanced back to where Rodger and his parents stood. "Nita couldn't make it. She and her kids are sick. So you ended up with two dates."

Tina mimicked Janet's earlier eye roll. Before she could spit out the retort reeling through her mind, Janet had moved back to Rodger. Tina let go a pent-up, angst-filled sigh and moved back to the empty chair between Drake and Jon.

After a few tense moments and what appeared to be a brief discussion, Rodger's father appeared, helping to seat his mother-in-law as Rodger pulled out his mother's chair. Rodger took the chair between his mother and Janet. Tina closed her eyes, sent a brief thank you heavenward, and pulled out her chair.

"Please let us help you," Jon offered. He eased the chair from her hands, pulling it out from under the table. Drake pulled her napkin from the table, shaking it out. Lord, the two of them acted like headwaiters at a posh restaurant.

Tina glanced at both. She took a quick breath, exhaled, and sat down, smoothing her skirt under her. Jon helped her scoot her chair up to the table, not before Drake laid her napkin on her lap. His hand lingered fleetingly on the outside of her bare leg closest to him. He smiled as she looked at him. Heat washed over her. She looked away only to find Jon watching her intently as well.

"Please sit down, gentlemen." Tina picked up her water glass and drank a third. As the coolness slid down her throat, she imagined a cool breeze wafting over her, hoping against the odds that Jon wouldn't reciprocate his cohort's action. No such luck. A warm, masculine hand snaked under the edge of her napkin. Strong fingers massaged the tense muscles under them.

Tina closed her eyes, willing her hand to not shake as she sat her glass down. Opening her eyes, she perused Jon from beneath her lashes. His gaze met hers as her eyes opened more. Someone cleared their throat. She looked to her right. Drake watched both of them intently. His smile grew as she turned her head.

Dropping her hands into her lap, she slid them along the top of her napkin until she felt theirs. She pushed against them while smiling and nodding as Janet introduced her bridal party from the head of the table.

Jon chuckled and leaned close, whispering, "I'll acquiesce for now."

Drake leaned in as Jon pulled back. "I'll behave for the moment."

Drake drank a quarter of the water in his glass. He smiled before pushing back his chair.

As Drake rose, Tina wiped her sweaty palms on her napkin.

"May I have your attention, please?" Drake's voice carried over the chatter happening at each table. He waited until a hush filled the room before continuing. Tina took the moment to enjoy eyeballing him close-up and letting her mind wander over his muscles and tight abs as her gaze reached his waist. Drake's massage and touch said he knew tacit and tactile. Tina gripped her napkin more. Images of Drake using those fingers on her flared across her psyche. More sweat coated her palms.

Tina willed her mind to change direction in thoughts, not that her hormones cared to obey. As her gaze moved back up Drake's torso, she caught movement out of the corner of her eye. Rodger's mother was glaring at her and shaking her head. Was the dragoness jealous? She could be all she wanted. Tina didn't care. Nothing was going on that anyone could tell. She bet the old bat and dragoness hadn't had sex since their last child was conceived. Rodger was thirty-one. Long dry spell by Tina's standards.

Drake raised his water glass and toasted the bride and groom. "To Rodger and Janet, may they find happiness and joy together. Now let the dining begin."

Drake sat down as he returned his glass to the table. Aunt Helen's mouth gaped, then snapped shut. Nathan hadn't wanted to open dinner. With Rodger tipsy and probably not remembering his rehearsed speech, Drake decided to take matters into his hands.

Besides, Tina looked and felt delicious. There was a part of her neck just below her ear begging for a nip and nibble every time she ducked her head as he caught her giving him the once-over. Fine by him. He liked a woman with an inquisitive nature.

As Tina ducked her head again, Drake looked over at Jon. Jon shot him a conspirator's wink and grin.

He hadn't staked a claim on Tina when Janet mentioned asking both of them to escort Tina for the evening. This was before Nita declined being a bridesmaid.

Sharing would be great. Jon could pleasure a woman as well as he could. Both of them would have Tina squirming when the time came. Planning and practice they didn't need, though practice did make perfect.

Jon stood, reaching for Tina's chair. He nodded to Drake. Rodger and Janet were heading for the buffet. Aunt Helen and the rest were making their way across the room to a similar set-up holding salads versus the hot entrees table.

Drake leaned down and spoke. "Tina, we're going to pull your chair out. Please wait until we're done before you stand."

Jon grinned as Tina shot him a quick look before she glanced at Drake. Her cheeks tinged slightly, as did places along her neck. He wondered if this was due to embarrassment or desire. Her fair complexion did little to hide either. An old memory flew across his mind. An old flame with similar fairness in the throes of passion flushed light red all the way down over her bust to her taut nipples. Would Tina prove the same? Jon swallowed and looked away. Many more sexy thoughts and his tight pants would display a hard-on that he didn't want to explain to anyone other than Tina, except maybe Drake, if a threesome happened.

As Tina stood, Jon let his gaze rove over her again. He liked his women soft and curvy. Muscles were fine, but rock-hard like a guy didn't feel right to him. Tina wasn't model thin nor was she obese. Her weight suited her without being obtrusive. He wondered what Drake thought. Drake recently commented on how he detested runway models who looked thinner than a warped board and had no shape to the point their clothes hung on them instead of complementing their figures.

Jon nodded at Tina as he glanced at Drake, hoping he caught his unspoken question. Drake arched an eyebrow and mouthed "what." Jon nodded at Tina again, adding a shoulder hunch for emphasis, and smiled as Tina turned to him. Drake grinned and nodded, mouthing "yummy."

Jon wanted to shake his head and cuff Drake on his arm. A boyish response to a grown man's reply wasn't worth the frustration and energy. Instead, Jon slipped an arm around Tina's waist and hugged her to him.

Jon felt and heard Tina's soft gasp. He winked at Drake and stepped away. Offering her his arm, he spoke. "Sorry to embarrass you. Some things are too good to resist. That was one of them."

"Embarrassing me was too good to resist?" Tina's tone and pitch left nothing to guess at. Jon looked to Drake who stood there shrugging and shaking his head.

"I'm sorry that came out the wrong way. I couldn't resist hugging you and touching you." Jon moved back, knowing that his dumb action could get him rejected for the rest of the evening. Crap, sometimes he reacted before he thought.

Tina's head dropped back as she looked up at him. Her red cheeks and demi-frown said she wasn't entirely convinced of his apology.

"Look, we all can make mistakes on first impressions. You caught me off guard, is all. Janet trusts you or she wouldn't have set us up." Jon watched Tina glance at Drake. "Well, set the three of us up."

Jon caught Drake's nod as Tina turned to face him. "Let's get food and drink while we can. Aunt Helen has a timetable she'll hold to if she has her way."

Tina nudged Jon with her elbow as she moved between him and Drake. "Don't stand there. Let's chow down."

Chapter Four

Tina returned to the table ten minutes later, followed by Jon and Drake. Each carried two plates with various food items on them. As Tina sat her plates down, a person dressed in a frilly formal gown stopped behind Jon holding three wine glasses and a wine bottle.

"Would you care for red or white?" The server placed the glasses on the table and showed the bottle's label. Tina knew the vineyard. The head dragoness scored points for choosing a local vintner for her purchase.

Tina didn't care which wine went with what. She knew what she liked. The red appeared dark and she could smell the tartness as the server began pouring. Jon picked up his glass, waving his over the top toward him. He sipped, swished the wine in his mouth and swallowed.

"Nice tart red wine. A bit of cherry, purple grapes, and other flavorings. I'm fine with this. Drake, you might want the white if it's sweeter. This is a bit dry, too." Jon held out his glass to the server.

As the server poured, she addressed Drake. "I'll be back with the white in a moment. And for you, ma'am?"

Tina knew she couldn't have more than a few swallows as she was driving home later. "I'll have a bit of the white when you return. I prefer seltzer with a twist of lemon and lime, please."

The server nodded and continued on down the table.

"Not much of a wine drinker?" Drake asked as he pulled out her chair, waiting for Tina to sit. Jon had stepped away to find them bread plates and rolls.

"I've enjoyed a bottle from the vineyard a time or two. I don't drink and drive." Tina quickly smoothed her napkin over her lap, hoping Drake hadn't noticed.

"I hope you aren't miffed at Jon's earlier slip. He's got manners. A bit of a nerd. I appreciate you not going off on him." Drake picked up his knife and fork after placing his napkin across his lap.

Tina nibbled on carrots and celery while she considered her reply. Jon had caught her off guard. Most of the men she attracted were decent and mannered. There were the horny toads from time to time. Between school and working full-time, dates didn't happen often. A quick cup of coffee with her male classmates didn't qualify as a date. Hell, her social life was nearly nonexistent thanks to Frank and his scheduling her extra shifts at the coffee shop. Money was tight and the additional cash paid for her classes. Her tact might be a bit off too. No, she didn't blame Jon. Maybe they could reach an agreement that would keep the old bat and dragonesses off them for the rest of the evening.

Jon set a glass of white wine in front of her. Tina looked up and smiled. She sipped some before she spoke. "Thank you, Jon. That is mild and sweet. I like the hint of blackberries as you swallow. The combinations they use to age and ferment mix well together."

Jon's smile as he sat down thawed the icy worry surrounding her heart. He didn't appear to be carrying a grudge. This interested her. Drake's defense of Jon made sense. Both men showed and expressed their interest in her. How they carried it off after tonight was another thing. For the evening, still four hours from ending, they needed a plan. Tina looked over to where Janet and Rodger sat, eating and conversing with people who approached their table. The dragonesses and old bat were busy holding court as guests and family members chatted with them as they refilled their plates.

Tina continued eating for several moments until two-thirds of both her plates were empty. Neither Jon nor Drake had made another move to touch or engage her in conversation. Both ate with gusto and asked if she wanted more before they each filled their plates a second time. As both reseated themselves, Tina wiped her mouth.

"I'm not mad at either of you over the earlier slip. With Rodger's mother, grandmother, and sister watching Janet's and my every move, the less we let on, the better off we'll be." Tina sipped more of her wine before changing to drinking seltzer.

Drake cleared his throat and raised his wine glass. "Here's to an evening without Aunt Helen keeping us under her thumb."

Jon laughed and clinked his glass with Drake's. "Here, here. To an evening free of Aunt Helen."

Tina couldn't resist either's infectious smile and wit. Neither one acted as though they had a vain bone in them. Each spoke confidently and appeared at ease with themselves and the night's festivities. She wondered about Jon, Drake and Rodger's friendship. Prior idle chatter about themselves revealed some of how connected they were. Before she let her guard down again, Tina wanted to know if anyone else was keeping score for the dragoness and the old bat.

"Aunt Helen? I didn't know any of Rodger's other groomsmen were related to him." Tina picked up her roll and tore a piece off. As she popped the piece into her mouth, Drake angled his chair toward her. He pushed his plates away from him.

"Only one of Rodger's attendants is a blood relative. His choices caused a nasty battle between his mother, grandmother, and him." Drake leaned back in his chair, picked up his wine glass, and drank. "Jon and I are the closest to family he allowed otherwise. The rest are old friends."

Drake paused in his conversation as servers reached between them to clear plates. Coffee cups and saucers appeared next with silver coffee pots. Cream pitchers and sugar bowls came next. Each table received a duplicate set up.

Tina held on to her seltzer drink until the table was cleared and the servers moved on. Setting her glass down, she glanced at Jon. "Care to elaborate on Drake's reply?"

Jon copied Drake's action, angling his chair so he faced her as well. He sipped his wine twice before he answered.

"Neither Drake nor I am related to Rodger. We're high school friends who attended the same college. My family lives four hours away. Drake's in another state." Jon sat his glass down. "We figure we spent enough time here as cousins would, so Mrs. Daniels became Aunt Helen. The mother hen neither of us wanted or needed."

Tina quickly sat her glass down, swallowing to keep from spitting her mouthful all over her. Jon's description of the head dragoness couldn't be more spot-on. She wondered if Rodger knew what astute friends he had. Tina smiled as she turned her coffee cup over. She reached for the pot close to her.

Drake stayed her hand. "That's decaf. Is that what you want?" He pointed to another pot close to Jon's elbow. "That's the real stuff. Both are vile to me. I asked for tea."

Tina slid her hand down Drake's arm until her hand covered what she could of his. She heard movement from Jon's side. Lord, were the two trying to outdo each other? Tina lowered her lashes and tried to look sideways to see what Jon was up to.

Warm breath caressed her ear and neck as Jon spoke. "Maybe a cup of half each is what you prefer. Which one gets the bottom, and which one gets the top?"

Tina gulped, unable to speak as images of Drake and Jon sandwiching her between them flickered to life and dimmed as rapidly as they formed. She blinked, hoping to catch the last one for later on as she drifted asleep, sated from breaking in her new vibrator. At least her dreams wouldn't be so cold and lonely.

Before Tina could reply, a throat cleared in front of them. Tina looked up. *Merde!* The old bat stood there glaring at them. Tina swore Mrs. Addams's eyes moved over Drake and Jon as though she was sizing up how to skin them and offer them up as steak tartar for the evening snack post-cake-and-coffee course.

Drake entwined his fingers with Tina's. He smiled, placed his napkin on the table, and leaned forward. "Yes, Grandmother Addams."

Jon laid his napkin on the table and stood. "Do you need help, Ma'am?"

Tina bit the inside of her bottom lip to keep from chortling. Mrs. Addams nodded, pointed to Jon and Drake, and walked off. A tinge to the old woman's cheeks suggested embarrassment, or her memories had ignited a fire that the old bat wasn't sure how to quell.

Drake raised Tina's hand to his lips. He slowly worked his fingers free from hers. As his gaze locked with hers, he dragged his fingertips across her palm, scratching lightly as he moved toward her wrist.

Tina clenched her legs and ass as Jon matched Drake's moves, except his fingers trailed down her arm, lingering in the fold her elbow made as she tried to raise her arm. Goose bumps rose from the top of her shoulders, down her arms, and across her chest until they reached her breasts, tightening around her already aching nipples. A deep breath wouldn't help. The bra she wore chafed her tingling skin with every breath she took.

She wasn't sure how much more she could withstand and not be obvious. As Drake rose, Tina looked around him. Janet and Rodger were nowhere in sight. As she looked around the room, breathing as deeply as possible, Tina caught two pairs of eyes glaring at her, Mrs. Daniels and her daughter. Crap! Double crap! The old bat must have spilled what she thought she saw.

Tina extricated her hand from Drake's. She blinked twice, working back the tears that threatened to overwhelm her. Tired and turned on didn't mix well. Neither did attempting to appease three women who needed to get fucked, re-laid, and so orgasmed-out that they suffered from a double dose of twenty-four-hour fuck syndrome and a few other things that she didn't feel like acknowledging in polite company. The polite company being Drake and Jon, along with Janet and Rodger.

"I think you better find Mrs. Addams. I need to find Janet and the bathroom." Tina moved to push back from the table. Drake moved behind her. He leaned down, brushed his lips on her cheek, and whispered in her ear.

"Whatever the woman wants can wait a moment. You can stay here if you like. Jon and I will make sure Janet comes to you. If you need to pee, I'll get you to the bathroom without having to deal with the crones from hell." Drake's voice swirled around her earlobe, warmed it, and disappeared.

Jon's voice warmed her other ear as he whispered his agreement with Drake's response. "I caught part of what Drake said. Don't let anyone belittle you. Rodger is keeping the peace for tonight. Tomorrow he'll blast his parents. Not all his friends and family are like his stick-in-the-mud mother, grandmother, and sister."

Tina offered the best smile she could given the turmoil brewing inside her. Janet didn't care what her future in-laws thought. She and Rodger openly discussed the type of household and atmosphere their home would be. Rodger wanted kids who played rough-housed with their siblings and their parents. Both he and Janet planned on pets. Their two rescue cats still fought with Rodger's miniature Schnauzer Tiny occasionally. Even Janet had declared two rooms of the four-bedroom house they were covertly buying as guest rooms for lengthy stays by loving, extended family members, a list Tina topped.

"Drake, I need some air. Could you get me to that bathroom while Jon finds Janet for me?" Tina rose and moved toward the open area behind her.

Chapter Five

Fifteen minutes later, Tina stood outside on the patio adjacent to the first-floor formal dining room. Drake stood talking with two of the extra help hired for the weekend at the far end of the patio closest to the driveway. Tina at first thought the pair had cigarettes in their hands until Drake pointed out the green glow of the items they held. As the hired help moved down the drive placing larger glow sticks along its edge, Tina snorted at her first impression of them paralleling what the dragons and old bat would have thought. Lord help her if those three were influencing her that strongly after a few hours in their midst. She turned back to where Jon and Drake stood, helping twist and loop together different colored glow sticks.

The awning covering the large outer deck and patio area twinkled and glittered as the glow stick chains fluttered in the breeze from the beach. The cool air felt wonderful against her flushed cheeks and neck. Tina pulled at the neck of her top, hoping to chase some of the air down her front. Drake and Jon talked amicably with the help stringing outside lights at intervals along the area's perimeter. Music softly played in the background as the DJ tested his system and soundtracks.

Behind her, Tina could make out bits and pieces of conversations that flowed over the hum of low-key discussions.

Volume said a lot about who talked and what they thought was important or their view of others around them. Tina smiled as she recalled her latest shift at the coffee shop.

Frank kept a sign behind the counter that asked folks to keep their heated discussions to a roar that needed no referee. Jack and Sam, two seniors and hard of hearing, often yelled a curse word at each other in challenge as they played poker and ate lunch. The two old codgers had misplaced their hearing aids and spent most of their recent lunch get-together yelling at the top of their lungs as they discussed sex at their ripe old age of eighty and what advice they needed to pass along to their grandson. Frank had turned red as Sam described in detail his recent sexual liaison with Mrs. Stinson. Tina later found out Sam's latest belle was Frank's grandmother. Tina swore Frank was going to be permanently red and ban Sam and Jack from returning.

Tina flexed her shoulders and stretched. She'd watched Janet go back inside after they briefly talked. Mrs. Daniels, Mrs. Addams, and Rodger's sister hadn't said anything about what they oversaw during dinner. Better safe than sorry was a motto Tina didn't take for granted. Janet agreed, forewarned allowed her and Rodger to stay ahead of the party poopers. Dancing would start soon. The older crowd would retreat to the upstairs library, where tables and chairs and a smaller dance area awaited them.

On the patio, contemporary music and a mix of nineties and eighties music rolled out of the speakers set up at various corners. Tina glanced at her watch. Its glow showed another forty minutes until the dancing began. She wondered how she would locate her car and depart well before midnight. As much as she wanted to stay and forgo working tomorrow afternoon, Tina knew she couldn't. Saturday dinner rush packed the shop and tips often equaled half another shift.

Tina pushed off the railing she lounged against and started down the three steps leading to the stone walkway near the driveway and the area where a valet attendant kept watch over the cars entrusted to him. He'd parked hers close to where the driveway curved around the back of the garage so she could drive around to the delivery entrance and make her way out to the main road without issue. The outside lights came on as she approached. The valet rose from where he sat. A box containing tagged keys lay on the table near him.

"Evening, Ms. Davidson. You're leaving early?" The lanky youth smiled as he reached for the box. "I can pull your car around if you need to get your things from the house."

Tina smiled, glad for the cover of twilight as she admired the young ass outlined by the tight black pants the valet wore as he bent over to retrieve the keys he dropped. Youth and exuberance once attracted her, but eye candy was great. She wasn't complaining one bit. Tina glanced over her shoulder as the valet looked away. Jon and Drake gathered near the DJ, talking with others who had wandered outside. Men with experience, tempered by wisdom and softened enough to know when to yield, fascinated her more. Men of her early thirties age group offered commonalities that enhanced their interactions and added enough more to the equation, increasing their attraction considerably.

She knew enough about Jon and Drake that they didn't worry her. Tonight was the first either had expressed an interest in her. Together, they ignited a fire deep within her that hadn't stopped smoking and smoldering since Jon hugged and kissed her. Drake's light touch and manners complimented Jon's nerdiness. The other times they interacted, Rodger's sister stood in for Nita who was definitely out now. Tina nibbled her lip as images of Drake or Jon dragged down the aisle due to their dragoness companion flashed through her mind. As humorous as the thought might be, Tina didn't want that to happen to either of them. How much persuasion would it take to let the three of them escort each other down the aisle without the dragonesses and old bat having a first-degree conniption fit? One more reason to convince Janet and Rodger to elope rather than let the dragonesses and old bat dictate.

"Right this way, Ms. Davidson." The valet spoke, pointing toward a section further back than where she remembered her car being parked.

While the young man appeared respectable and without reproach, Tina wasn't taking chances. She nodded and turned toward the patio. "I'll be right back. Excuse me, please."

Tina quickened her step without waiting for the valet's reply. She wanted Drake or Jon with her when she checked on her car. Both would be better. Out of prying eyes would also give her a chance to verbalize her interest in them both and see if their intent matched their words. Keeping things low-key until they could act without repercussion mattered. Tina wanted Janet to enjoy her party as well as impress her future in-laws. Tina needed to give a message to Drake and Jon from Rodger. If the message meant what she thought it might, more fireworks than those planned for the midnight hour were on tap. Too bad she wouldn't be around to see the extra entertainment.

Tina picked up her pace as she got closer to Drake. "Drake, can I talk to you and Jon for a moment?" Tina raised her voice to be heard over the increasing volume of music coming from the speakers close to them.

Drake moved toward her, nodding, holding his hand out to her. Jon held up his hand to the person he was talking to and walked toward her. As Drake reached her, Tina took his hand. Warmth flowed over her, and a sense of safety enveloped her. Jon came around her other side and slipped his hand into the crook of her arm. Heat moved off him as though he marked her. The feeling of rightness doubled in strength. Tina sucked in air and tried to swallow her uneasiness. Reacting to these two this rapidly unnerved her some. It wasn't like she'd agreed to go to bed with them. Not yet, her conscience crowed.

Willing herself to take slow, deep breaths, Tina cleared her throat, wet her lips, and spoke. "Janet spoke with Rodger. He's done with biting his tongue and his mother's dictates. He said to tell you to keep an eye on things out here for now."

Drake smiled and nodded. "I wondered how long he would last. Did he deliver the message himself?"

Tina looked at Jon, seeing if he had anything to add. He shrugged and shook his head.

"Not all of it. I got the last part from him directly as he joined Janet and me briefly. She informed me of their short discussion as his father escorted his mother upstairs to the library." Tina squeezed Drake's hand as she slid her arm free from Jon's hand to place her other hand in his.

Drake squeezed back as he leaned down and brushed his lips over her cheek. "Aunt Helen's a control freak about keeping up appearances. I'm not surprised at his message."

Jon nibbled her earlobe quickly before he kissed her cheek. "I'm glad we're out here and nowhere in earshot when he delivers his message."

Tina snorted and tugged on their hands. "I need to check on my car as I'm leaving around midnight. The valet pointed to an area that is not well-lit. I'd appreciate you coming with me to locate how I'm going to get out of there."

Drake scrunched his face into a worried look that was almost comical. His lips puckered like he wanted to kiss her, and with his eyes squinted as he arched his eyebrows, he reminded her of a kissing gourami fish she saw at the aquarium.

Tina bit her lip to keep from laughing as Jon moved in front of her, mimicking Drake's look. He grinned and nodded. "I'm game. Drake might be afraid of the dark."

Drake chortled, cuffing Jon on the shoulder as he replied. "Darkness doesn't scare me, bro. It's Tina leaving that has me perplexed."

"I've got to work tomorrow. Some of us have bosses who insist on us putting in our time to get a paycheck." Tina tossed her head back to get a better view of Drake.

"Just because I own my business doesn't mean I don't have to punch a time clock, too." Jon cuddled closer to her as he leaned down, continuing. "My business partner offered to take the weekend for me so I could be here. Running a repair garage isn't exactly a nine-to-five venture."

Drake cleared his throat. "My office runs an open leave policy. I can make up my hours by telecommuting on the weekend as needed for my clients. Marketing creativity faces a few restrictions."

Tina loosened her hand from Drake's. She reached up and tucked loose strands of hair behind her ear. "I'm sure your boss loves your dedication. I wish mine paid better and would hire some additional help."

Drake bobbed his head in understanding. "Looks like *we* need to find you a better job."

"We—" Tina began, cut off as Jon spoke.

"Let's find your car and figure out how you'll get out of here. I wish you didn't need to leave." Jon walked forward, still holding her hand.

Tina followed Jon, still stinging from Drake's remark. As much as she knew networking led to new jobs, Drake's tone and emphasis on "we" sounded like he wanted to dominate her. No man or woman got the privilege after her parents. God bless their departed souls. Both had taught her and her siblings by example and experience to stand independently as necessary. Tina wanted someone who partnered, not someone who saw her needing constant care or direction. She wasn't a mindless ninny. Drake's remark aside, she still wanted him. Could they reach a compromise and enjoy their shared desire?

Chapter Six

D rake watched Jon walk away with Tina. Drake fought the urge to cuff himself upside the head over his lame remark as he made his way across the patio. That didn't stop the incessant laughter of his ego or the egging of his conscience either. He knew the age of chivalry died eons ago. Manners hadn't. How could he apologize and sound sincere? That would take some doing.

Drake trotted down the patio steps and onto the walkway, hoping to catch up to Jon and Tina before they disappeared around the garage corner, where the valet pointed as Jon and Tina spoke with him.

"I'm sorry, Ms. Davidson. I moved your car closer to the loop around the garage so you could get out easier. When the lights came on, I noticed the ones on the side of the garage didn't light up." The valet held out a flashlight he'd turned on. "Best I can do until someone checks on the lights."

Jon took the flashlight. "It's okay. Not your fault. I'll let the Daniels know."

The valet's weak smile strengthened as he offered Tina her keys. "If you need to move your car, go ahead. No one else is heading out before you. Even the DJ is crashing here. Great gig when you get fed, paid top wage per hour, and a place to crash, too."

Tina nodded as she held her hand, palm up, to the valet. "I hope you get tips, too. Those help to offset the taxes."

The valet laughed and saluted her. "So far, I can't complain. Dinner was good. Not bad music. I get to drive some fine cars. Don't worry about tipping me. Ms. Morton took care of that when she arrived."

Tina slid her key ring onto her middle finger and closed her hand around the keys. Sure she wouldn't drop them this way, she moved up behind Jon. Glancing over her shoulder, she noticed Drake's approach. "Jon, let's wait for Drake."

Jon looked over his shoulder, his lips near hers. Tina stood on her tiptoes and pressed her lips to Jon's.

She pulled back quickly, not wanting to give the valet fuel for gossip. Help talked no matter what they were told. Spreading rumors or malicious statements made no sense to her. She was blessed with fast, true friends and few acquaintances that dwelled on what they considered juicy fodder about others. She heard her share at the coffee shop.

Drake reached them as she rocked back on her heels, regaining her balance. Drake mouthed, "I'm sorry," and rested his hand on her shoulder. Tina knew he wanted and needed some kind of reply. He had to wait. She wasn't giving the valet any more to think about. Best she could do for now was to acknowledge Drake. "Glad you caught up with us. We're going to check on my car."

"Thanks. I'll tag along and see what help I can lend." Drake moved up beside Jon. "Lead the way. I'm right behind you."

Tina felt Drake's hand cup hers that held her keys. He let go after a slight touch. A fleeting thought came to mind. Was he being standoffish until he knew his apology was accepted? She would let him know soon enough. Check car first, apology issue second, and hot hugs and kisses third. Tina hoped she didn't glow too badly as they moved out of the valet's view and into the maze of cars moving toward hers.

Ten cars back and another five over, they found her car. Jon shined the flashlight on the license plate. Tina, glad for the cover of dark, realized the double entendre her personalized plate might be interpreted as. FOX8LDY was not too hard to understand. The sticker on the rear bumper, right above the plate, read, "Coaches do it better." Understanding slammed through her on why she got quite a few horn honks and grins as people passed her. Janet insisted on placing the bumper sticker on the car. Tina hadn't connected the two until now. Jon's low whistle pulled her attention back to them.

"I say you got a problem." Jon crouched near the passenger side's rear tire. He panned the flashlight beam over the tire and down toward the ground. Tina sucked in air as he ran the beam along the ground.

"Flat tire. Not a big issue. Drake and I can change that for you easily." Jon rose and faced her. "How's your spare?"

Drake inched his fingers along her palm, clutching the keys. "I'll get it out, and we can have this done before the dancing starts."

Tina clenched her hand tighter around the keys. She caught her top lip between her teeth, worrying it as she scolded herself and figured out how to answer Jon's question. There was no way around it. She'd done the one thing her parents had taught her never to do since she started driving. Admitting it verbally panged her more than she cared to admit.

"My spare isn't." Tina inhaled and let go of the angst-filled sigh she'd been holding back. Her mechanic had reminded her to get the tire replaced. Funds hadn't permitted five new tires. She was paying off the four from two years ago and her recent inspection charges. So much for getting her air conditioning fixed.

Jon leaned against her car and clicked off the flashlight. "Let me get this right. You don't have a spare?"

Tina closed her eyes, swallowed, and resisted nodding. Jon couldn't see her reply if she did. "Yes, I don't. I need to replace it. My mechanic refused to let me have the one I had back. He said the donut was too fribbled to allow it any road time. Trying to find single tires for this car is hard and costly."

Drake slipped his arm around her waist and hugged her. "Older sport cars are notorious for that."

"Thanks, inheritance from an uncle. Low miles and good condition made upkeep easy until my other car bit the dust." Tina leaned into Drake's embrace. He tightened his hold on her and relaxed. His arm lay loosely around her waist with his hand cupping her hip. His fingers traced its curve as if he traversed familiar territory.

Jon came to her other side and placed his arm around her shoulders. He gently squeezed and released, moving a step away. "I can help. If you don't mind..." Jon's voice trailed off.

Tina palmed her keys in her hands, deciding what to do. She needed a way home and to work. Taking the bus the ten blocks to the shop she could handle. Getting home provided the catch. The sporadic evening schedule left her no choice but to walk home. Blast it, why had she waited to grocery shop?

"I guess," Tina started. Drake kissed the top of her head, distracting her.

Drake offered his suggestion. "We'll both help if you like."

Tina shrugged. "I've got to work tomorrow. Getting me home is one thing. I've also got personal stuff to do."

Jon clicked on the flashlight. "Let me call the shop. I can get your car towed to the garage. A friend specializes in sports car detailing and repairs. I bet he's got the tires you need in stock."

Drake moved around in front of her. "I've got my mom's car while she's out of town. I can loan you mine until Jon's got yours road ready again."

Tina transferred her keys to her least sweaty hand. She wiped the empty one on her skirt and reached out for Jon's. "You got a deal. Please keep the cost as reasonable as possible. I appreciate you doing this."

Jon took her hand and turned it over, palm up. He raised her palm to his lips. He nibbled the fleshy part near her thumb, worrying the area near her wrist before he pressed a line of kisses into the center of her palm. As he raised his head, he curled her fingers in, capturing his kiss. "You're welcome," he whispered.

Drake held his hand out. "Let one of us take the keys for now. We'll be sure the valet knows what's going on. For now, I think you need a hug." Drake worked her keys out of her hand as he continued speaking. "Don't worry. We're in this together."

Jon slipped behind her, clicking the flashlight off as he did. "Together we're going to see this through. And a hug is what we all need right now."

Tina could feel Jon's breath on her neck as his warmth radiated across her back. His arms slid around her waist, tugging enough to make her stumble backward to him. Balmy didn't fit what she felt as he settled her against him. Every breath each of them took brought them together. Nothing overt happened. Neither was the scalding desire pouring off him on to her concealed. Tina inhaled deeply, willing her eyes to not close as Drake moved in closer.

"Since my eyes adjusted to the darkness, I'm seeing better. And seeing you in Jon's arms looking at me is very, very enticing. I think Jon's right, we all need a hug." Drake's voice lowered to a husky murmur as he moved closer. "Delicious."

Tina tilted her head back to gaze at their faces. She could make out shadowed images of Jon's face as well as Drake's as his hand laid on her hip, stroking downward and back up. With each stroke, he inched higher, moving along her belt and just below the waist of her skirt. As his hand roamed higher, he bunched her shirt in his hand, shoving it up until he found flesh.

Tina tried to keep her eyes open. The moon illuminated the outline of Drake and Jon as they leaned in, cradling her between them. As she turned her head to the left, she exposed part of her neck. Her lids slammed closed as Jon's lips found and traced her ear with his tongue. He nipped and laved, worrying the edge of her ear as he worked his way toward her earlobe.

Drake inched his fingers under the hem of her shirt, dragging his finger nails along her exposed stomach. He traced the outer rim of her navel before working the pads of his fingers up her ribs and along the edge of her bra. His other hand rested on her, above her waist, not quite near her breast. His breath swirled around her ear, mingling with Jon's as Drake pressed his lips along her bare collarbone.

Tina didn't know whether to pant or attempt deep breathing to calm her racing heart. Either way she came in contact with Drake and Jon. The more she leaned into Jon, evidence of his desire rubbed against her ass. Drake touched full bodily as he cupped both breasts and nipped her throat. His hard cock rode against her as he slightly moved his hips while murmuring against her flesh what he would love to be doing with her.

"I would love to feel you climaxing hotly as we got you to come repeatedly." Drake lifted his head, withdrew his hands from under her shirt, and kissed her cheek.

Tina rocked forward, going up on her tiptoes. She threaded her hands into Drake's hair and pressed her lips tightly against his. Her tongue traced the outline of Drake's lips, seeking entrance. Drake opened his mouth as a loud cry was heard over a pause in the music.

"*You're eloping?*" Mrs. Daniels's voice carried out over the brief silence and any further words were drowned out by the noise blaring out of the speakers closest to the house.

Drake stepped back, shaking his head. Jon's exasperated sigh spoke volumes. Tina tugged her shirt down and tucked more loose strands of hair behind her ears.

Chapter Seven

"Let me guess, the fireworks have started," Jon forced out, tugging at his breeches, hoping to gain composure. He scooped Tina's keys out of Drake's hand and tossed them in his waist pack.

"Christ, Rodger never gets his timing right. Thank god Janet is with him." Drake combed his hands through his hair.

Jon held up his hand as he turned on the flashlight. "One of us is going to have to brave the dragon lair and see if we can calm things down a bit."

"Right," Drake began, snorting as they moved back toward the patio. "Whose job is that? Aunt Helen is going to be furious."

"Excuse me, I got a question." Tina's voice rose and drowned as they passed the speakers at the patio's edge. The DJ put on music that called for a slow dance. Several of the couples present chose partners and began swaying with the ballad playing.

Drake motioned her to him as they reached the table area further away from the speakers. "Yes, what's up?"

"You call Mrs. Daniels's aunt. Are you related to her?" Tina's voice still had the huskiness from their passionate exchange. Drake blinked and willed his id to calm down, like that was going to easily happen. Jon's suppressed smile didn't help. Damn him and his ironical wit. Double damn Rodger for announcing to his mother about his elopement. Eloping meant doing it without telling folks.

Jon's snicker broke Drake's chain of thoughts. "I need Tina with me to call the shop. I'll be with you in a few. Go scout ahead without bearding the dragonesses or the old bat as best you can."

Tina nodded and started toward the door they'd come out of earlier. She stopped and called out over her shoulder. "I'll get my stuff and meet you back here. Maybe we can use calling the tow truck and my flat to get us out of here."

Drake wanted to crawl under a table and wait until the two returned. He wasn't afraid of Aunt Helen. But how did he tell the woman who considered herself his second mother she needed to butt out of her son's life and realize he'd grown up? Did Rodger have the balls to even broach the subject with her? Drake rolled his shoulders, pushed his sleeves up, and followed Jon and Tina into the house.

"Aunt Helen isn't a blood relation," Drake offered as he caught up to Jon and Tina. "Rodger and we grew up together over the years. In college, we reconnected after our parents had moved around during high school."

Jon turned as they reached the patio doors leading into the house. "Since here was closer than going home a lot of times, we ended up here for breaks and lesser holidays. Aunt Helen co-opted us to the point of introducing us as her adopted sons."

"Oh, I bet that went over like a lead balloon," Tina spit out, trying to keep her mirth in check.

"Lead is the key word," Jon agreed. "Our parents finally put a halt to her mother-henning even them on how to raise us considering we were eighteen and legal."

Tina moved up beside Jon and faced Drake. "So Aunt became her honorary title?"

"It was the only one that shut her up when the argument between all the parents started one Thanksgiving. By then a couple of distant cousins from each family had married and united our families." Drake moved in front of the door. "How are we going to pull this off?"

Tina glanced around Drake. There weren't many people left in the dining room. Janet was talking with several of Rodger's cousins. An idea formed as Tina scoped out the rest of the room from her vantage point.

"I'll get Janet's attention. That will get my cell and tote bag from upstairs. That way I can have them with me due to us waiting for the truck to arrive and I need to go with them." Tina smiled as Jon nodded in agreement.

"I can use the house phone to call without being questioned. I'll meet you back here in about ten minutes." Jon slid the patio doors open and sauntered inside heading toward the kitchen.

Tina lingered near Drake. "What are you going to do?"

"Dare the dragoness's lair and hope she isn't breathing fire. Rodger's timing still stinks. What is Janet doing down here if he's telling his mother he's eloping?" Drake's mouth opened, closed, and opened again. No words came out. He squinted, shook his head, and sighed.

"Might be he's not the one telling her?" Tina shrugged and followed Jon inside.

Drake shook his head again. Who the hell was eloping?

Drake followed Jon and Tina into the hallway separating the dining room from the kitchen. Janet looked up from where she sat talking with one of Rodger's elderly aunts. The woman was in her nineties and still spry. She told Janet more than once, well within the hearing of Aunt Helen, that it was time Rodger moved out and got going with producing his own family. Whatever else the aunt said, Drake didn't know except several women walked away from the group with their cheeks tinged.

Janet smiled and waved as they approached. Jon veered left, heading toward the kitchen and the phone there. Tina threaded her way through the ring of chairs, stopping to say hello and touch the shoulder of a few of the women. As Tina reached Janet, Drake glanced around the room. The crowd appeared to be thinning out. More were making their way upstairs to the library. He could hear strains of music in between beats of the rhythms playing outside. Thank God the house faced toward the shoreline. Complaints would be few if any since most of the Daniels' neighbors were almost a quarter mile away.

Drake waded through the group until he reached Janet and Tina. He worked his fingers into Tina's clenched hand, hoping his touch would help center her.

"I've got a problem," Tina said as she faced Janet. "My tire is flat."

Janet's eyes widened as a frown creased her mouth. "How did...when...shit, now what do we do?"

Drake willed his reply to stay trapped in his mouth. The last thing he needed was another idiotic blurt coming out. God, when had his hormones taken control and his logic fled?

Drake squeezed Tina's hand as she looked at him. He smiled and spoke. "May I?"

Tina nodded, squeezing his hand back. Good, he'd saved them both embarrassment and kept his macho ego quiet for a bit longer. Desire could snap back and explode at any moment. Getting and keeping his lusty id under wraps would take more time. Concentrating on the issue at hand made cooling off easier.

"Jon owns a repair shop. He's calling his dispatcher to send a tow truck. Since Tina's spare is..." Drake grabbed his side, glaring at Tina.

Tina smiled up at him, batting her eyes coyly as his sister used to do when she'd act innocent after tattling on him when their parents left him in charge. Drake muffled his groan, attempting to smile through the sharp ache spreading across his side. He leaned down and whispered in Tina's ear. "You got one lethal elbow, woman. That hurt!"

"Sorry," Tina murmured. "Janet's got enough to deal with. Let me handle this, okay?"

Drake rubbed his side and nodded his agreement. If nothing else happened tonight, he was learning more about Tina than he and Jon knew before. She held her own, gave as good as she got in many of their interactions, and had better manners than some of the people attending the party. There was depth to her that many missed due to their own shallowness. Drake could see why Janet and Tina were besties. He bet they had history and tenure like his and Jon's long-standing friendship. Rodger aside, Jon was his longest friend, closer to him than his two brothers, and the one person he implicitly trusted next to himself.

Tina cleared her throat and spoke. "My spare is dead. I never replaced it when I got new tires."

Janet glanced at Drake. He looked away. He knew that look all too well. Surprise and ire mixed to simmer without exploding to a blowout. Drake swallowed any retort or response he had. This was between Janet and Tina. He shrugged and pointed over his shoulder. "I'm going to check on Jon. He's calling the garage to get the car towed."

Janet licked her lips as she watched Drake walk away. She moved closer to Tina. "I'm not going to dignify your car trouble with an 'I told you so' comment. I'm glad Drake and Jon are helping you with the issue."

"You know so am I," Tina said. Her voice sounded tired and edgy. Janet wished she could take Tina upstairs and both of them climb into bed after a hot shower each. Rodger's mother and sister were upstairs in the library holding court. That wasn't going well from the chatter coming from folks as they came back down and made their way out to the patio.

"Mind if I change the subject?" Tina asked, reaching up to rub her neck and temples.

"What's up?" Janet noted the dark circles forming under Tina's eyes. Also the earlier glow in her eyes was not there. Damn Frank for not hiring more help. Blast Tina for not taking the office job offer she'd gotten two months ago.

"Are you eloping?"

Janet opened her mouth, closed it, and gripped Tina's hand. Janet swiftly moved across the room, excusing herself as she practically dragged Tina behind her. Halfway across the room, Janet dropped Tina's hand and spun around.

"Shit," Janet ground out through clenched teeth. "I wish you hadn't asked that in front of Rodger's elderly aunt. The woman has a tendency to ask the most direct and blatant questions."

"She's the one that's hard of hearing?" Tina stepped closer to Janet. "Not the aunt that asked Rodger's mother if she forgot how fun sex was?"

Janet clapped her hand over her mouth, trying to muffle her giggles and keep a case of hiccups at bay from stifling her mirth. She fanned herself with her other hand while sucking air in through her nose. Several deep breaths later, she dropped her hands to her side and faced Tina.

"Not that particular one. Her twin sister who is an eagle eye tattletale and reports on everyone as she thinks she's the matriarch of the family."

"Crap, I'm sorry." Tina touched her shoulder, heaved a deep sigh, and tossed her head back. "Tonight's been a weird mix of hot and cold stuff happening."

Janet nodded and leaned closer. "I overheard that Rodger's sister is the one who's eloping." Janet looked over her shoulder at the stairs leading to the second floor library. "Kerstin's announcement wasn't well received either. Bad enough she drops the bomb at Rodger's party. Kerstin told her mother that if she thought she was planning another fiasco like this she could put those plans where the sun didn't shine and pointed to her ass."

Tina covered her mouth with one hand as she held up her other hand between them. Her fingers were spread like in their teens to show a high-five score.

"Oh yes, I wanted to yell 'score' and high-five Kerstin. But at that moment I was here and she was up there braving the dragoness's lair.

Janet smiled, raising her hand with fingers spread. Their hands met as Tina's other hand dropped from her mouth.

Chapter Eight

J anet snorted as a door slammed loudly. Mrs. Daniel's voice carried down the stairs, drawing everyone's attention. "Kerstin, open this door."

Janet moved to the center of the room and rapped on the wooden table near her. She rapped again as she glanced around the room. Most of those present faced her. "I'm sure we've all had time for our food to digest. Let's head out to the patio to enjoy dancing and see what other desserts the caterers laid out."

She walked over to Rodger's elderly aunt and offered her arm. "Aunt Esmeralda, shall we see if that chocolate tart you talked about is out there?"

As Aunt Esmeralda rose, Janet caught Tina's gaze. Janet nodded toward the double doors and smiled. The group began moving pairs toward the doors. The sooner they got them out of earshot the better off the evening might end.

Tina moved toward the head of the group. Janet sighed as she steadied Esmeralda. The woman had to be in her eighties. Her friendship with Rodger's college suitemate Stuart's Grandma Getty indicated Janet's guess couldn't be too far off. Esmeralda and Grandma Getty shared a birthday. Neither allowed more than one candle on their joint birthday cake. Either woman would share a bout of gossip, laugh, challenge the other to juice it up more, and then scold the other for not being juicy enough.

Janet returned Esmeralda's smile as they made their way through the patio door and out on to the deck where several couples sat. More chairs joined the others and with the help from many of the younger men present, a few tables joined the seating area, providing space for partaking of refreshments.

The DJ turned the volume down and asked anyone who needed it lowered more to let him know. Soon a slow bluesy piece filled the air. Several couples meandered out on to the deck and began dancing. Janet turned and spotted Tina lounging against the open doors. One of Esmeralda's friends offered to take care of getting her settled. Janet thanked her and quickly moved toward Tina.

Tina's shoulders slumped as she pushed off the door. Janet knew that posture too well.

"Are you okay?" Janet asked, closing the space between her and Tina.

Tina shook her head. "I'm worried about the cost of car repairs and my tight budget. Then there's the ongoing battle burning upstairs." Tina jerked her thumb over her shoulder pointing toward the house.

Janet nodded as she reached for Tina's arm. "I agree. Best we can do is to keep out of the line of fire. Where are Drake and Jon?"

"Still inside. I'm going to check on them."

As Tina turned in the direction of the door, Janet grabbed her arm and lightly tugged.

"Let me handle them and what's going on. I'll send them out to you shortly." Janet glanced over her shoulder. Esmeralda was waving. "Can you see what Esmeralda needs while I take care of things?"

Tina's slow reply worried Janet more. Her finances must be pretty tight for her to be this distracted. Janet nudged Tina, getting her attention back on the current state of affairs.

"Yes," Tina began, stopping to muffle a yawn. "Go on. I've got it covered."

Janet stepped into the house. She began making her way to the kitchen as loud voices echoed down the stairs.

"Mother, I will not let you decide for me. I'm grown." Kerstin's terse pitch left no room for guessing. An all-out war was seething, ready to erupt. Janet shook her head, wondering who was more of a control freak at the moment, Kerstin or Mrs. Daniels. It didn't matter any longer because this was not supposed to be happening. Janet looked up, deciding whether to intervene or leave well enough alone, when she spied Rodger sitting on the loveseat near the dining room fireplace. He seemed to be staring at the floor.

"Rodger," Janet began as she approached him. "What are you doing?"

Rodger looked up and shrugged. He held his hand out to Janet and spoke. "Thinking about doing the same thing Kerstin announced to mother. Except..."

"Except what?" Janet didn't like the way Rodger's voice trailed off. "We've got enough going on without you being vague, too."

Rodger stood up, threading his fingers in between Janet's as he took her hand. "We aren't going to tell them. Kerstin's been spoiling for a fight ever since you and I got engaged. Well now she's got it. Mother and she can work it out or not."

Janet blinked. She wished she could knock some sense into Rodger concerning his family. Letting his mother have her way on some items hadn't solved anything. She and her entourage kept pushing and taking over more. Janet knew that loving someone didn't mean you always agreed with them or understood them. Right now, she didn't know who plucked her nerve more, Rodger or his mother. Janet inhaled slowly and exhaled a silent sigh.

"I strongly suggest you find your father and get this under wraps. I've got the guests outside. I've got to find Drake and Jon." Janet yanked her hand away from Rodger's. "Do you think you can handle that?" Her tone took on a pissed off pitch as she narrowed her eyes, hoping her glare and growing ire came through without her needing to add volume.

Rodger opened his mouth, ready to retort she was sure. Instead he glared back at her, stuck out his tongue, leaned down, brushed his lips over hers, and walked away. Janet clapped her hand over her mouth to hide her smile. No, it was hanging open. Damn, he'd actually caught her by surprise.

Rodger stopped halfway up the stairs. Turning, he spoke. "I agree with you on part of this. Letting Mother make a fool of herself might be worth the fall out. But..."

Janet nodded, waiting for him to continue.

"But embarrassing everyone is not an option. Also, this is our moment. Not mother's or Kerstin's. At least Grandmother is in her room complaining of a headache." Rodger smiled and trotted up the stairs.

Janet dropped her hand, hoping she didn't burst into laughter. She didn't know or care where Rodger found the grit to confront his mother and sister. She hoped he took reinforcements with him as he entered the dragoness's lair.

Janet turned into the hallway leading to the kitchen. The closer she got, she picked up on a conversation happening between Drake and Jon. She paused outside near the kitchen entry.

"Drake, you know I wish fixing Tina's car was easy. Tires are going to be special order I bet." Janet could make out Jon's profile as he leaned against the sink.

"I can't say. Your specialty is cars. Mine is advertising. Your mechanics are top notch. I'll back you on that. You've fixed my cars more than once without trying to find add-ons like other mechanics might." Drake's gentle tone and confident pitch eased any lingering apprehension Janet had about the two men's integrity. They genuinely cared about people. Janet smiled at Drake's next statement.

"Doing right by Tina is something you and I do 'cuz its part of who we are. Our ethics don't wave in the wind. Neither you nor I could back away from her without feeling regret and angst over it."

Janet caught Jon's smile as she entered the kitchen. "Hey, Jon," Janet responded as Jon's smile grew at seeing her. His megawatt beam reached his eyes. No doubting his sincerity.

"I got a question for the two of you," Janet offered, pivoting on her heel so she faced both Drake and Jon.

Drake rose from where he sat on a stool near the breakfast counter. "Sure. What you got for us?"

Janet glanced at Jon before she spoke. His gaze met hers and didn't look away. Good, one more reason she trusted the two with her best friend. Tina needed good men in her life and these two fit that description.

"You two want what's best for Tina, right?" Janet wet her lips, braced for their reply and willed her mouth to remain shut no matter what they said until she heard both of them out.

Jon moved closer until he stood next to Janet. He spoke with a subdued voice. "I want to help Tina. I'm attracted to her. That isn't why I'm helping. I'm helping because that's who I am."

Drake leaned in and added his reply. "Yes, I want what's best for Tina. I'm attracted, too. Neither of us is going to make a move without her consent. Like Jon said, we're helping because we care and want to."

Janet held up both thumbs to each. "Good. I've got other things to deal with. I need to know she's gonna get home safely."

Drake and Jon both nodded as Drake spoke first. "No problem on that. I promise you she'll be fine. I've offered my other car to her. Jon's making arrangements to get her car towed to his garage."

"Thanks, guys. Tina's out on the patio looking after Rodger's elderly Aunt Esmeralda. Rodger and I will be out in a few. Maybe you can take turns dancing with a few of the unpartnered women." Janet winked as she began to pass by Jon.

Jon cleared his throat, stopping Janet. "I want you to know we're going to take great care of her." Jon shot Janet a thumb-up. "Now go take care of what you need to. We'll check in before we leave."

Janet nodded and picked up her pace as she exited the kitchen. She'd hoped to find one guy for Tina. Finding two was more than she planned on. Working things out was up to the three of them and not her place to meddle in more.

Jon waited until Janet exited the kitchen before he spoke. "I hope the truck gets here soon. This evening has turned into weirdness extraordinaire."

Drake glanced over his shoulder and around the kitchen before he replied. Jon wondered if either of them knew how much the dragoness and her cohorts observed. Fallout would be what they decided to turn their narrowness and opinions into. Made no sense to let them ruin what was left of the evening.

"I've got a feeling that Rodger is baiting or waiting for his mother to focus on something other than him." Drake shook his head and pushed off the counter he leaned against.

Jon chuckled, nodding in agreement. "Let him deal with the fallout. We have a lady waiting for us. I think some dancing and cuddling is a great way to spend time until the truck arrives."

Jon waited until Drake started down the hall to follow. Neither of them wanted to be within earshot if Rodger and his mother started arguing. Her tactic for roping others into the fray wasn't going to work with them. Rodger was on his own.

"I say let's take the side door out to the main deck from the hall. Avoiding the volcanoes erupting upstairs makes a lot of sense." Jon almost bumped into Drake as he halted near the door in question.

"Remember as kids we use to think there were too many doors on this house? I'm glad for them tonight. Escaping makes good sense." Drake gave Jon a thumbs-up and opened the door.

Music rushed in as the door swung open. Jon caught sight of Tina standing near two of Rodger's elderly aunts, engaging them in conversation. She nodded and smiled. Her fisted hands opened and closed as the two aunts chattered away without stopping. Time to rescue their lady had come.

Chapter Nine

Drake looked out over Jon's shoulder. His gaze found Tina as she looked up. Even at this distance, he could make out her semi-smile and watched her posture change. Subtle differences that most wouldn't notice. Drake knew people sent out silent messages that many missed. Body language and nonverbal cues were important in advertising. He'd developed a passion for people watching and reading them. The one rule he kept foremost and tried to not deviate from was checking in. Verbal discourse remained important and a necessity to ensuring understanding.

Drake nudged Jon. "Tina looks ready for a break. Rodger's aunts are chatterboxes. Their interests are varied but sometimes the topics aren't on par for every generation."

Jon snorted. "With their ribald sense of humor, we both know they won't hesitate to ask who Tina has the hots for more, you or me."

Drake slapped Jon on the shoulder. "Okay, smart ass. Are you going to take bets on that?"

Jon turned partly toward Drake. "Why not when I already know the outcome? We're tied for first place."

Drake chortled and shoved Jon out the door. "Come on, let's go rescue Tina. We'll decide who gets the first dance in a moment."

Jon stumbled as he hit the first of the two steps out onto the deck. A slow dance piece from the seventies pulsed out the speakers. The volume was noticeably lower than earlier. Good thing, too, as more couples were swaying together and making their rounds as they danced close together.

Jon glanced at his watch as he stepped onto the deck. At least another hour per his dispatcher until the tow truck arrived, possibly two. 9:45 p.m. Not late and not evening any longer. Tossing his head back, Jon caught the stars in the dark night sky overhead. Somewhere in the distance, the surf could be heard pounding the shoreline. In between drum beats, the chirps of crickets made their presence known. A couple of dances with Tina in his arms and two watching Drake with her would end the night with positive feelings.

As Drake moved up beside him, Jon raised two fingers. "Two dances each? Who goes first?"

"Sounds good. Well I'll rescue and you find out what the DJ's got that doesn't require disco moves." Drake started to turn. Jon stopped him.

"Disco? Neither of us is wearing tight pants and I gave up those moves long before graduation." Jon winked as he gave Drake his cheesiest grin.

Drake pointed to the DJ. "Grade school antics I don't need reminding of. You want to fast dance, fine by me. I want slow and cuddly. Up close cuddly."

"I'm on my way. So I guess that leaves out the Bee Gees and Donna Summer on the playlist." Jon resisted the urge to put his thumbs in his ears and wiggle his fingers at Drake. Talk about grade school much less junior high antics and responses.

"Dude," Drake groaned. "Let's not show our age, shall we?"

Jon smiled, pressing his lips together to keep his merriment in check. There were dances and music to attend to. Banter could wait.

Drake watched as Jon walked away. Growing up, the two of them fought like bitter enemies from time to time. Even bickered over who was Rodger's closest friend. In the end, their camaraderie brought them together and cemented their friendship to the point each trusted the other implicitly. Theirs was a best-friend friendship neither would break nor take for granted.

Drake made his way across the deck to the patio. He smiled as he overheard Aunt Esmeralda's comment. "Victoria Getty bet me a month's worth of poker money Stuart and Joanna would get married before Rodger and Janet. Damn if the old gal didn't call that one right."

"Stuart is married." Drake stopped in front of Esmeralda. "Last I heard he and Joanna eloped while on vacation in Vegas."

"You heard right. Victoria isn't happy with them. She wants a church wedding. We'll see what comes of it." Esmeralda attempted to stand. Drake offered her his arm. "Thank you, Drake. How did you find out about Stuart?"

"His cousin Abebi is my boss's staff assistant." Drake steadied Esmeralda as she straightened her jacket and smoothed her sleeves. "Where are you headed, Aunt Esmeralda?"

"Where I can watch the dancing and get me a drink. My throat gets dry gossiping." Drake laughed as Esmeralda elbowed him.

"Tina, don't believe a word she told you about me or Jon. We're angels." Drake helped Esmeralda to another seat close-by, near the refreshments sitting on the patio picnic table.

Esmeralda's throaty laugh deepened Drake's smile. He stepped back, shaking his finger at her. "Behave and no making up more gossip."

Esmeralda patted his arm and nodded. "I think Tina needs a drink, too. I'll entrust her to you and Jon."

Esmeralda's last words drifted away as a burst of wind blew across the patio. Drake inhaled sharply as she finished her last statement. He looked around and most of the women appeared to be watching the dancing. If any heard her, none indicated this. Drake bent down and kissed Esmeralda's cheek. He whispered in her ear before up righting himself. "Behave yourself. Jon and I will take good care of Tina."

Esmeralda's knowing smile and wink tickled Drake. He bit his lip to keep from laughing. He winked in return. Drake faced Tina and held out his hand.

"How about a drink and a dance?" Drake asked. He moved closer to Tina. He could feel her gaze move over him. It was almost as though a silent communication happened between them. She nodded, ducked her head, and came up smiling, reaching for his hand.

"Sure, why not," Tina responded.

Drake took a hold of Tina's hand. He tugged a bit as his fingers wrapped around hers, pulling her closer to him.

"Why not is because I've waited to do this for hours." Drake leaned down and brushed his lips over hers before she could protest.

"Hours," Tina quipped. "All right. We'll discuss that later."

Drake tightened his hold on Tina's hand as she tried to pull away. "Dance first, then drink. I hear my request starting."

The opening strains of "Open Arms" by Journey began. Drake led Tina on to the dance area and slipped his arms around her waist. He slowly snaked his hands over her waist and back until they met in the small of her back. He eased into her until he brushed against her. Her full breasts rubbed over him, sending currents of electric desire bolting deep into his groin. He knew better than to even bring their nether regions into proximity, but he couldn't resist.

Since sandwiching her between he and Jon, need and want simmered like a watched pot ready to boil over. Behaving he understood. Propriety he would observe since this was Janet and Rodger's night. For the turn of a dance, in the shadows near the edge of the area, he could let the steam between them fuel their mutual desire.

Tina swallowed hard as Drake rubbed against her breasts. Her nipples pebbled, begging for more with each swipe. Raising her arms to loop them around his neck, she put herself in direct contact with him. God, the intimacy felt so good and absolutely right. His foot moved in between hers as his hands moved to her hips and rocked her to him. His waist met hers and his groin nestled on her mons. Need welled up in her. Lord, her vibrator was going to get a good work out tonight.

As the song continued, Drake moved them around the dance floor only separating them as they came into light. Once they entered the shadows again, he pressed fully against her. Tina licked her lips and looked up. Drake watched her intently. The need to kiss him sparked as the guitar crescendo built in passion. The musician couldn't have known how his song would affect his audience. Tina glanced to her left and right. They stood still well out of sight of the others. Drake's back was to them. Tina closed her eyes and puckered, rising on her toes as she did.

Drake's partly opened lips met hers. His tongue teased her until she bade him enter and the tasting began. He deepened the kiss as he worked his hands over her hips and up to her shoulders. Two more sips and they broke apart as the last refrain of lyrics and music faded into silence.

"Here's another oldie from the eighties by the Police, 'Every Breath You Take.'" Drum beats rolled out of the speaker near them.

Tina smiled up at Drake as he looked into her eyes. She inhaled deeply as she thrust her shoulders back. He laughed, causing his chest to rub against her. Tina sighed and closed her eyes.

Comfort and safety weren't words she expected to use concerning Drake this soon. They fit what she felt. No others came to mind.

As the lyrics continued, Drake swayed them across the floor and back to their corner. More kisses and caresses happened as they cuddled up to each other. Another turn across the deck found them close to where Jon stood. His smile and nod along with his outstretched hand puzzled Tina. She looked up at Drake and blushed.

Jon burst out laughing. "I don't want to know what brought that on. I'll just see what I can do to add to the fire."

Drake cuffed him on the shoulder as he leaned over and whispered. "She kisses real good, and dances exceptionally well."

Jon retorted, "Kissing and telling, eh? Tsk, Tsk. Maybe I'll let her compare notes and ask who is the winner."

Drake shook his head and tucked Tina's hand into the crook of Jon's arm. "Your next dances are claimed. Jon likes to dip and twirl so keep your eyes open and your thoughts about you."

Jon watched Drake walk over to the closest chair and sit down. His eyes met Jon's and neither of them blinked. Jon knew Drake shared and yet this time there was a possession going on that said "mine" without blatantly saying so. Jon didn't care, because in the end, together, they knew Tina desired each of them. Drake smiled and made a twirling motion with his hand.

"We've got the dance signal," Jon said. "Let's enjoy some cuddles, shall we?"

Jon waited for Tina's acceptance, either spoken or nonverbal. She nodded as the next dance piece began playing. The slow easy rhythms and melodies of Kenny G flowed out and surrounded them.

Jon entwined his fingers with Tina's and moved in closer, leaving some space between them. He laid his hand loosely on her waist near her hip. Catching her gaze, he turned, bringing her with him. He preferred to dance as his parents and others of their generation did. Rather than making out with their clothes on, they danced. Not dirty dancing or the arms around necks, bodies up close way either. They allowed space and air between them. Jon wanted to pull Tina tight to him and feel their mutual heat envelop them. He knew that doing so might bother her and he preferred to stir his own embers into blazes of passion tonight. Feeding off Drake's earlier arousal of Tina would be great if they were working together, however, they weren't. Jon wanted to see how he and Tina reacted to each other.

As they moved toward the corner on the opposite side of the deck, Jon slid his hand along Tina's waist until he held her in the small of her back. Her breathing rippled under his hand as she exhaled. On her next breath, he pulled her closer to him. A soft sigh and gentle "hmm" escaped her as she bumped up against him. Jon swayed them in place as the music repeated several bars of the chorus. He leaned down and blew along Tina's neck, working his way close to her ear.

Chapter Ten

Tina fought against closing her eyes as Jon blew along her jaw. She knew giving into the desire flooding her nether region and pumping back up to her taut nipples, she'd not stop at one kiss. Two, then three, maybe more. Her fingers itched to thread themselves through Jon's hair and massage his scalp as they shared one French kiss after another. Drake had ignited a fire that wouldn't burn out. Jon blew on the banked coals that the pause between dances as she changed partners allowed to cool.

How much more any of them could withstand and not throw caution to the wind? That couldn't happen. Janet and Rodger deserved respect regardless of what the dragonesses thought and did. And now the shit storm with Kerstin's revelation added fuel to a bonfire ready to explode out of control.

Tina turned her head as Jon reached her ear and pressed her lips on his. There was no denying her need to kiss and touch him. Taking advantage of the brief time they had in the corner made her decision all the more daring. Tina moved tight to Jon and ground her hips on him. His sharp hiss and groan said more than if he'd verbalized his reaction. The man's desire rolled off him and right onto her. Talk about lighter fluid and combustible need and want. Tina worked her fingers loose from Jon's. She trailed her nails up his arm until she reached his shoulder. His sleeves kept her from knowing if she affected him much. She dragged her other hand up over his abdomen and over his pecs until she felt his hard nipple beneath her fingertip. Lightly she drew two circles around it before he grabbed her hand and dragged it back down below his waist. Nestling her hand palm up between them, he rocked against her, nudging and rubbing. Tina smiled as she tossed her head. Jon's erect cock provided her answer. He was aroused.

As Jon began to turn them back toward the light for another foray across and around the dance floor, his cell phone rang.

"Shit," Jon started. "I've got to answer this. It's the shop's ring tone."

Tina drew in two deep breaths and counted. At least her desire wasn't as evident as Jon's. He reached down and quickly tugged his crotch back into a lower rise. He then fished his cell phone out of his waist pack. He covered the mouthpiece as he spoke. "Go sit with Drake while I find out what's going on. I'll be over in a moment."

Tina made her way across the patio, skirting the couples still dancing. As she reached Drake, he stood. Concern filled his eyes. He started to speak as she held up her hand.

"Jon sent me over. His phone rang. It's the shop calling." Tina combed her fingers through her hair, working hard to regain her composure. The night might be ending soon. She needed to know what to expect as far as her car and getting home was concerned.

Drake scooted over on the bench he sat on. He patted the space next to him. "Sit down. I'm sure Jon will update us as soon as he gets off the phone."

Tina sighed as she sat down. "Yes, I'm jittery about my car and getting home. I've got to work tomorrow."

Drake raised her hand to his lips. He brushed his lips across each knuckle before turning her palm up and pressing a kiss into it. He closed her fingers tight on her palm.

"Hold on to that tight. That is a promise kiss. A promise that you will get home okay and have a car to get to work."

"Thanks, but I can't afford a rental car. And cabs are not cheap." Tina swung her legs back and forth as she glanced at Drake. His calm and reassurance helped some. The not knowing was the worst.

"No rental car. No cabs either. I've got an extra car that needs driving. Jon garages my parents' car while they are out of the country. They won't mind you using their car. Besides, my mother would insist." Drake slid his arm around her shoulders, hugging her to him. "And neither Jon nor I are going to leave you to fend for yourself. Please know we're here to help. All right?"

Tina swallowed her comeback remark about taking care of herself. She knew she needed help. Janet and she both talked about how stubbornness and pride didn't always solve things. Time had come to accept Drake's offer and trust her earlier feelings. As she danced with Jon, similar feelings flowed through her. Janet had remarked shortly after their first introductions to each other that Drake and Jon were two of Rodger's better friends. Others couldn't hold their own with the dragoness and her cohorts. Tina smiled at her last thought.

As Tina turned toward the door thinking about going back in to check on Janet, Rodger and Janet stepped through the door. She wondered how Janet was doing.

Janet carried two bags with her. Tina recognized one. Where had the other come from? Tina excused herself and walked over to Janet.

"Thanks for getting my bag and purse," Tina voiced as she took the tie-dyed tote that practically matched her outfit. She peered inside, checking for her regular purse. Her small strapped clutch hung from her waist. Drake still had her keys.

Janet shoved the other bag at her. "Here, this is yours, too. Remember you brought the extra bag with your stuff just in case you decided to stay?"

Tina arched an eyebrow, blinked, and wet her lips ready to reply. Janet winked and spoke further. "Take that with you so I don't have to worry about it."

Janet motioned her closer. Tina leaned in to hear Janet whisper. "Put the bag in my car. You've got the key in the inside pocket of your tote. Rodger and I are escaping behind you."

"You're eloping?" Tina glanced right and left to make sure no one except Janet heard her.

"Quiet. We're not sure yet. Rodger sicced his father on his mother. The two of them are heatedly discussing something behind closed doors. Kerstin stormed out twenty minutes ago taking a cab somewhere. Grandmother is snoring loudly out cold on her bed. We got the door open to check on her."

"Wow, not a great ending to your wedding shower." Tina took the other tote from Janet. "I'm sorry things turned out like this."

Rodger moved back to them after talking with Drake and Jon. He leaned close to keep the volume of their conversation low. "Jon's tow truck will be here in thirty minutes. We'll check on things and make sure that all is under control. Once they leave, we'll make our escape."

Janet clapped her hand over Rodger's mouth. Both shot Tina a look that said "Mum's the word." Tina wondered how many times she could hold back retorts without making a permanent indentation in her tongue with her teeth.

Better to know what Rodger and Janet might decide than not knowing. Tina shrugged and spoke her less sarcastic and tired thoughts.

"I wish you well whatever you decide. Right now I want as little drama as possible for the rest of the evening. Is there any way we can make our way over to the valet and the cars without everyone watching us?" Tina held her hand up where Janet and Rodger could see it and jerked her thumb toward her shoulder. "A few are watching us right now probably wondering what's going on. They're going to know soon enough when the tow truck gets here."

Tina startled and jumped as Drake reached in taking a hold of her hand. "Sorry to interrupt folks. Jon and I were talking about how to do this without a lot of rubbernecking going on."

"I'm wondering the same thing," Tina said. Her patience couldn't stand much more wear and tear. Her game face was beginning to sag more than she cared to let on. Too many things going down at once and many of them beyond her limit to care. Time to take care of herself was rapidly taking priority.

Jon moved up opposite Drake in the huddle. Jon cleared his throat. Tina looked up and saw the others were attentive on Jon. He gave a single nod of his head and spoke. "The truck is going to draw enough attention taking the car out and also possibly messing up the lawn. I think Tina riding out with me is the best option. Down the road we can switch so Drake can take her home. We'll deal with car issues in the morning."

"I've got to be to work at ten. That doesn't leave much time for sleep and sorting out car issues. There's got to be another option," Tina countered, ready to wring her sweaty palms together. Stifling yawns and tiredness got harder the more she had to concentrate on multiple items.

Janet stepped into the middle of the group. "Here's a way we can all get out of here. Jon, you follow the truck with your car. Drake, you're following Jon to take him home once he drops his car off at the garage for Tina to use in the morning. Rodger and I will take Tina home."

"What about me in the morning?" Tina let go a long exasperated sigh. Soon her angst was going to win and come out in borderline assertiveness that edged into aggressiveness. Patience was a virtue she was running low on.

Quiet filled the air in the circle of five. Tina glanced at each of the other occupants. All eyes were on her. Lord, had she sounded that shrewish already? She swallowed, ready to apologize when a loud crash echoed out the open patio and deck doors. Two voices yelling and screaming at each other followed. Rodger groaned and rolled his eyes. Janet clapped her hand over his mouth. Drake and Jon almost spoke in unison, "Oh Lord, they're at it again."

"I want a divorce," Rodger's father called out.

"Well so do I," his mother replied. "Except this time, I'm following through. You'll hear from my lawyer in a few weeks."

"Fine, until then you sleep in the opposite end of the house and see if I give a damn." Rodger's father stormed out across the patio and into the door for the guest wing of the house.

Rodger pulled Janet's hand off his mouth. "Christ, I'm not staying here to settle this tonight. Mother is on her own. Come on, Janet, let's make our way out toward the cars. Tina, you ready to make a dash if needed?"

As Tina opened her mouth to speak, bright lights illuminated the opposite side of the driveway. Bright flashing red and yellow lights topped the truck pulling into the drive. Jon stopped before moving to greet the driver. "Looks like your cover is here. Let's get this going and we can decide while they load Tina's car what to do in the morning."

Twenty minutes later, Rodger pulled out past his mother standing in the middle of the deck waving her hand. Janet turned back to Tina as they got to the main road. "I'll get you to the garage tomorrow as we discussed to pick-up Drake's parents car after work. Be ready for me to pick you up around nine-thirty."

Tina nodded as her eyes slowly closed. Sleep demanded its time and place. Her mind put out the shut sign as her breathing deepened.

Chapter Eleven

3 *days later*
Tina reached over and poked the sleep button on her alarm clock. The ringing grew louder the more awake she got. She pulled her pillow over her head. Leaving an open space to breathe, she closed her eyes, willing herself back into the scalding hot dream she was having. Silence happened and she smiled as she caught fringes of her dream before it passed into the nether regions of her mind. A loud click sounded, followed by her answering machine picking up. Her greeting message barely finished before the one voice Tina did not want to hear came bellowing out the speaker.

"Tina, this is *all your* fault. Pick up this phone and talk to me *now*. You know where Janet and Rodger are. Stop hiding and answer your phone." The machine cut off as Mrs. Daniels paused. Tina didn't know whether to applaud or write a thank-you letter to the manufacturer. For now, the woman was gone.

And so was her sexy dream cuddled between Drake and Jon.

Tina tossed back her covers and sat up. She blinked as her eyes focused. Across the room, the answering machine blinked at her. Normally the volume was turned down so she slept through the ring of the kitchen extension. Tucking her hair behind her ears, she picked up her glasses. Her last pair of disposable contacts lay torn in their case. Impatience and Frank's blathering had pushed her farther than she ever considered before. The extra shift had turned into ten hours straight on her feet. Ten hours of rushing around serving coffee and food mixed in with nursemaiding Jack and Sam along with Frank's prattle about her ten-minute-later arrival fueled her decision to quit. She wouldn't announce her imminent departure until she knew she solidly had another job.

Yawning as she stretched, Tina shoved her feet into her slippers. Her robe lay across the foot of the bed where she'd left it two days prior in her haste to dress and get to work on time. Thursdays, her usual day off, she puttered around the apartment in her pajamas doing what she wanted. This Thursday she couldn't afford the luxury. Job hunting demanded she get busy sending out resumes and following up on her interviews prior to Janet and Rodger's wedding shower. Besides, if she turned off the ringer on her landline along with the volume on the answering machine, if Mrs. Daniels called back she could yell all she wanted. Tina wouldn't and couldn't hear her. A huge smile grew as Tina contemplated the idea.

Tina drew on her robe and dropped her cell phone into the robe's pocket. All her job leads and interviews had her cell phone number. As Tina crossed her living room, she paused by her computer. An envelope with Janet's handwriting leaned against the monitor. Tina picked up the envelope, opening it as she made her way into the kitchen. She tossed the envelope on the table close to the countertop coffeemaker. Smoothing out the pages a few moments later as her coffee brewed, Tina read the first page. She laughed and continued reading. By the time she reached the back of the second page, Tina had her hand over her mouth.

Tina, both Rodger and I knew this might happen.

Well, it did. We eloped. By the time you, our parents, and the rest of the wedding party get this, we'll be in Vegas, hitched and heading to San Diego for a two week cruise for our honeymoon. Don't worry about the pets.

My neighbor is taking care of them. We'll be in touch when we get back.

Hugs,

Janet

Tina shook her head. No wonder Mrs. Daniels wanted to know where Janet and Rodger were. The pleasant surprise was Tina didn't know any more than anyone else. Great for Janet. She'd trumped the dragoness and her sidekicks. Sure, there would be hassles when they got back. Tina would love to see the look on Mrs. Daniels face when Rodger finally told her off.

Tina reached for a mug as both her cell phone and landline rang. She cut the ringer off on the wall extension, pulled her cell out, and checked the caller id. Jon's number showed as the phone chirped again. Tina pushed answer and greeted Jon.

"Hi Jon. How's things?" Tina bit her lip as sounds echoed in the background before Jon spoke. He was at the shop. This had to be about her car. Muffled words sounded and Jon's laugh warmed her ear.

"Hey lovely. Hope I didn't wake you." Jon's voice came through as if he were next to her. Tina tugged the neck of her top, fanning air over her bare breasts and nipples beneath. They begged for attention as memories of his good night kiss and caresses before he left after their first date two days ago.

"No, you didn't. Mrs. Daniels did." Tina pulled out a chair and sat down.

Jon's low whistle caused her to hold the phone away from her ear. She missed part of his next sentence. "...won't stop until she gets what she wants. None of us know which cruise they booked."

Tina laughed as Jon continued. "Drake is ready to rename Aunt Helen, Madame Barracuda."

"I couldn't think of a better name myself," Tina offered, bursting out in laughter.

Jon's merriment mixed with hers for a few minutes before he spoke again. "I got news on your car."

Tina gripped her phone tighter. She'd found her last repair bill and the bottom line had emptied a good portion of her savings that time. Tires alone were going to run at least three hundred.

"Remember I said I wanted you safe and that meant thoroughly checking your car out." Jon paused as though he wanted her acknowledgment.

Tina swallowed, reminding herself to breathe, and responded. "Yes, both you and Drake reminded me I couldn't put off repairs after he talked with you."

"Well, darlin'," Jon began. Tina loved the bit of southern drawl Jon's voice took on when he called her that.

"Go on. I can handle it." Tina stood and grabbed a pencil from the drawer close to her, ready to write down the information Jon gave her. She turned the open envelope on the table over.

Jon rattled off three items and stopped. "I could do more but I'm not the domineering type. The cost of fixing the brakes, oil change, and flushing your transmission is five hundred. I ordered your tires from a wholesaler I do business with. We already discussed their cost."

Tina wrote down the balance in her savings plus what she had left in checking until Frank paid her next week. Figures didn't lie. The repairs added up to more than she could afford.

"Jon, is all of this..." Tina began.

Jon interrupted her before she could finish. "Tina, all of its important. Your brakes and tires wouldn't pass inspection if it were due. And your transmission needs cleaning so I can check out the gear box for the five-speed and clutch."

"It's more than I can," Tina stated, swallowing her pride and finished speaking, "afford at the moment. Can it be done in stages?"

"Parts and tires will be here at end of the week. I might have a way you can get this done and help me out, too."

Tina held the phone away from her ear. She looked at the total she'd circled next to the amount Jon quoted for her tires. She licked her lips as the smell of fresh coffee filled the air. Her stomach growled. She'd consider Jon's idea over breakfast and get back to him. "What you got?"

Jon's voice lowered in volume and got warmer in tone. "My bookkeeper needs time off. Her granddaughter is due any day. How long she'll be gone is up in the air. I need help until she gets back. Invoices and receipts along with making the bank deposit every few days. Her software system is simple."

"Are you offering because you feel sorry or really need the help?" Tina pressed her phone tighter to her ear, hoping Jon's reply was the latter.

"I'm feeling sorry for me." Jon's nervous laugh set off butterflies in her stomach. Why was he feeling sorry for him?

"You got me wondering why." Tina picked up the pencil she'd been writing with and started doodling next to her figures on the envelope.

"Cuz I don't get Hyacinth's damn computer software. I do better at fixing cars and managing the shop. She'll teach you what you need to do. Please say you'll help out." Jon's throaty sigh warmed Tina more than she realized. She picked up the envelope and started fanning herself.

"Sounds like you need help defending yourself against the computer," Tina joked. Jon's soft laugh eased her apprehensions about saying yes to his job offer. The extra cash would help with paying for the repairs and let her say no to Frank's perpetual offer of extra hours.

"Yes, please save me from that awful machine." Jon's smile came through without even seeing him. His warm tone and upbeat pitch urged her to say yes even more.

Their date had gone wonderfully. A picnic dinner on the beach watching the sunset over Cascade Bay rivaled the patio dining the restaurants along Shore Drive offered. The walk along the surf as the stars filled the twilight sky overhead highlighted a wonderful quiet evening talking about the party as well as getting to know each other more. Jon had asked her to date Drake as well. Jon felt guilty about taking her out alone.

Drake's prior work commitments kept him from making the evening a trio date. She felt curious and relieved that both appeared open to their being three and yet seeing each other separately.

"Since you asked so nicely, I'll save you from that dastardly software." Tina began laughing before she could ask when Jon wanted her to start.

"Thanks for rescuing me. Seriously, Hyacinth needs three to four hours to bring you up to speed. How about tomorrow morning you and she get started? Please." Jon's easygoing emphasis on please solidified Tina's decision. Jon and Drake's courteous nature remained intact regardless of the situation. The issue with getting her car into gear when the tow truck arrived tested their mettle with regard to curse words and courtesy. Jon mentioned the Shakespeare phrase mug on his desk more than once during his stint under her car getting the gear shift unstuck that evening.

"Tomorrow sounds okay. Frank will have to get used to me not being at his beck and call. I need to check my schedule for the rest of the week to let you know when I'm available otherwise." Tina jotted a note on the envelope about her schedule. "I'll get back to you after I check my calendar."

Jon snorted. "Drake wants me to upgrade my cell phone to one of those smart ones. I told him I don't need to look something up when I'm under a car up to my elbows in the poor thing's guts."

"I understand that. I rely on paper and ink. Sometimes I forget to charge my cell phone," Tina replied as a loud beep sounded. "Either my battery is running low or I got another call coming in. I'll call you later when I got my calendar in front of me."

"Thanks, Tina, I appreciate you rescuing me and Hyacinth." Jon quickly hung up before Tina could say good-bye. She smiled as she glanced at her caller ID. Drake's number showed next to the time. Eight-forty-five AM. Tina's stomach growled as she answered.

Chapter Twelve

"Morning delicious." Drake's greeting had Tina reaching for her top and fanning herself again. When had talking to someone gotten close to producing sexual chemistry? She hadn't seen him since he stopped by the coffee shop to drop off the keys to his parents' car. The night before turned out short on relaxed sleep. Her dreams filled and flowed around Jon and Drake, fueling her desire and need.

"Morning yourself," Tina tried to not squirm as the heat rolled down her, settling between her legs.

"Your phone rang several times before you answered. Everything all right?" Drake's concern came through loud and clear with his husky low tone directed for her rather than at her. How did he do that? What was he doing as he talked to her?

Tina fanned herself more, plucking the hem of her top and moving it in and out. Her nipples grew tauter and pushed against her soft cotton top. Every rub, pull, or move on and over them sent ripples firing off in different directions. She reached for the hem of her sleep shorts, hoping to let cooler air in. No such luck as she tugged, she pulled the waist higher and the seams of the crotch tighter against her.

Drake's voice broke her concentration. "Tina, are you there? I asked have you eaten. Have breakfast on me?"

"Bre–breakfast on you," Tina stammered. Visions of Drake nude, laid out on the bed with raspberry jam smeared on a certain part of him teased her as her libido tried to take control.

"Sweetie, I think you need food before we try where your mind is at." Drake's warm laugh pulled her mind back to balance on the edge of sexual fantasy and primal need dictated by hunger which smelling the fresh coffee wasn't helping.

"Oops. Sorry." Tina fanned herself again. This time with the envelope near her neck and face.

"No need to be sorry. My thoughts possibly parallel yours in many ways. Let's get some food in us and talk about where we want to move us forward." Drake yawned before he continued. "I need about forty minutes to shower, dress, and meet you somewhere."

"Me, too." Tina stood, stretched, and wandered over to the window looking outside. The sunlight shoreline glistened as the tide rolled in along the beach. Pristine blue skies dotted with a few clouds greeted her as she gazed toward the restaurants dotting the commercial area of Shoreline Drive heading into Cascade Bay city limits. "How about I meet you at Chadwicks? The breakfast buffet is scrumptious and downhome cooking. I know the owner Tilly. She cooks a mean steak and eggs combo if you are a large breakfast eater."

"Sounds good to me. I missed my morning workout due to a late night at the office. Nothing that good food and a lovely lady won't banish. Well, some coffee, too." Drake's laughter and poking fun at himself helped banish her uneasiness that he caught her and understood where her mind loitered.

"Thanks for equating me with your morning workout. I haven't exercised you yet." Tina clapped her hand over her mouth. Where had her control gone? Out the door and run off as her great Aunt Mabel used to say when Tina spouted off as a child.

Drake's chortle deepened the heat she knew was already reddening her face and neck. "Hon, I'm sure that will come in due time."

Tina glanced at the clock on the wall near the backdoor. She estimated what time she could easily meet Drake at Chadwicks. "I'm going to let you go for now so we can continue this conversation face to face. See you at Chadwicks in fifty minutes?"

"You bet, babe. And Tina?" Drake drew her name out as visions of him stretching nude as he lay stretched out on her bed crashed through her mind.

"Uhmm—yes Drake." Tina reached over and turned off the coffeemaker. Nothing like the smell of burnt coffee to banish her fantasies.

"Mom and Dad said use the car as long as you need to. They're spending two months at their Hawaii condo. Dad is glad someone is driving the car rather than it sitting." Drake blew her a kiss over the phone and hung up before she could reply.

Damn, both of them had caught her off guard. How bad did she have it for Jon and Drake? Bad needed changed to good. Her interest and desire hadn't reacted this much since her last relationship two years ago. A broken engagement and bruised ego were the least of the effects the idiot left. Learning to trust herself had taken time and healing. Healing hadn't come easily. Trust remained stronger than she realized. Janet said it best. Trusting herself meant feeling and acknowledging when her subconscious nudged her. The nudge this time showed the message with the word forward and two thumbs up.

Tina picked up the envelope off the table and made her way toward the hall leading to her bedroom. Partway down the hall, she paused. Her hair frizzed in different directions. The belt to her robe sat cattycornered around her waist. Her pajama top was shoved up enough to expose part of one breast. The waistband to her sleep shorts mimicked the position of her robe belt. There was no doubt she reacted to Jon and Drake. Either one turned her on and piqued her interest. Together they stimulated her. Could she handle both together at the same time if things got as hot as her dreams and fantasies had?

Tina did an about-face and quickly entered her bedroom. At the rate she was going, a cold shower wouldn't even begin to put a damper on the heat streaming off her. Maybe if she focused on why she was meeting Drake her temperature might cool off some. As she tossed clothes on the bed, she wondered what Drake's opinion of Jon's job offer would be.

Disrobed, she turned on the shower to cool. No need to show up with chattering teeth dressed in sweats with the outdoor temperature in the middle eighties.

Drake pushed off his bed and on to his feet. His cock stuck out, blocking his view as he glanced down. Not a bad reaction to his dreams and hearing Tina's voice.

He took a deep breath and moved into the bathroom. Showering might cool things down.

With the water set at tepid, Drake entered his shower. Jets pulsed out the walls as the showerhead sprayed water down on him. The marble-tiled floor caught the water, swirling it down into the drain center of the floor. Drake slicked his hand with shower gel and began lathering his unaffected areas. His cock bobbed and begged him to pick up where he left off. Need shot through him as he bent over to wash his legs. Water caressed his balls and ass, sending tendrils of heat deeper into his groin. As water sluiced over him, visions of Tina on her hands and knees with Jon on his back with his legs spayed, fondling his cock in front of her. Tina's head lowered as she reached for Jon. Drake swallowed hard.

Jon's elicit groan pulled him deeper into the fantasy spinning before him. Drake glanced over Tina's shoulder watching Jon lever his hips off the bed and thrust in and out of Tina's puckered lips. Jon fisted his hands in Tina's hair as he picked up the pace. Her head bobbed in counter rhythm to his movements. It was as if his cock never left her mouth.

Drake knelt on the bed between Tina's legs. He leaned over her, brushing his lips down her shoulder blades, slowly nibbling, and licking her soft skin. Drake reached down, working two fingers into and out of Tina. Her juices coated his fingers as more joined the plentiful source. Easing his fingers in deeper, he found her fleshy G-spot and began to stroke.

Tina moaned as she loosened her mouthful of Jon. More moans filled the air the more Drake rubbed and fondled her fleshy bud of need. He moved closer. Tina pushed back against him, groaning as he thrust his fingers in and out of her. Tina tightened around his fingers. She rocked back and forth, making throaty noises of pleasure. Jon urged him on. Drake watched as Jon began stroking himself faster. His gaze focused on both of them.

Drake eased his fingers out of Tina. He quickly tore open the condom pack near Tina and eased the condom over him. He grasped Tina's hips and pressed against her.

Chapter Thirteen

Drake closed his eyes as he sank slowly into Tina. Heat greeted him. Tina's movement slowed as she groaned and panted. Her pitch changed as he pushed forward.

"Easy, love," he soothed. "Let me take it slow and easy."

He grasped her hips firmer, steadying his entry. More heat enveloped him the deeper he got.

Tina ducked her head and moaned deep in her throat. Drake slid up to his balls deep in Tina. A pounding need boiled in his balls as he pulled back. On the next thrust, he—

Drake rocked back on his heels. His eyes shot open as his own orgasm raced up his cock. He groaned loudly as the first spurt of jizz sprayed out. He stroked up and back, using the oozing fluid to coat him more, allowing extra friction to heat his need to come once more before he could think beyond bringing Tina home to spend an hour or two soaking balls deep in her. One last burst of orgasmic energy looped around him, tightening his swollen balls close to his perineum as his last surge of semen spilled forth.

Drake soaped his body again, clearing off the last dribbles of jizz oozing out of him. He inhaled slowly as he reached for the cold water spigot. Soon a chiller rinse sloshed over him, taking any heat and sexual drafts away from his main focus.

Ten minutes later, Drake tossed his towel into the hamper behind the bathroom door. He whistled as he shaved. He paused as he rinsed his razor, wondering what made getting ready for this date different than others. Was it the anticipation of building up to his fantasy?

He finished shaving and dressing as he pondered his reaction to the women he dated before Tina. Some were thin and curvy in a model sense. Others were heavy and flirtatious in their own right. Maybe the difference was her attitude toward Jon as well as himself. She didn't fear her attraction to both of them nor the idea of being involved with both. Drake nodded as he combed his fingers through his hair. Monogamy didn't work for him. Jon knew that, too. They tried it and failed miserably.

Drake smoothed his shirt into the waist of his belted jeans. He glanced at the socks he'd tossed on the bed as he laid out his clothes. The idea of strolling the beach boardwalk after breakfast came to him as he listened to the weather report. Sneakers and socks full of sand would detract from focusing on Tina and any discussion they might have. Drake grabbed his deck shoes, sat on the bed, and pulled them on. As he tied them, an idea formed. He'd have to talk to Jon first. Tonight might be their first trio date and an evening of seeing how they responded to each other together.

Another fifteen minutes rolled by before Drake rushed out the door, car keys in one hand and stuffing his wallet in his back pocket with the other. He laughed as he backed down his driveway. Tina got him daydreaming and hornier than any other woman had in quite some time.

Tina pulled into the last parking place near Chadwicks. She inhaled as she opened her door. Fresh cinnamon buns filtered through the air, tantalizing her nose. The next fragrance following was fresh ground coffee with a hint of hazelnut blew off the exterior coffee stand near the patio seating entrance. Tina licked her lips and looked for Drake's car as he got out. Two parking spaces over, she spotted him standing by his car, shielding his eyes with his hand as he held his cell phone to his ear. Tina waved as she slung her purse over her shoulder. Drake returned her wave and began walking toward her.

Tina made her way to the patio entrance. Her favorite server, Jorge, greeted them. He sat them closest to the corner where the noise level was lower. Drake ordered steak medium well with scrambled eggs, an English muffin, and one of the cinnamon buns they saw another table served. Tina winked at him as he asked what she wanted. "I'll have Tilly's three-egg omelet special. Hold off on the cilantro on top, instead a dollop of mango peach salsa, please. Sourdough toast with her homemade butter and blueberry preserves. Add another of those cinnamon buns, too, please."

Drake smiled as the server asked if they wanted iced coffee or hot. The temperature read eighty on the bank billboard across the street. Ten o'clock and the heat level indicated another scorcher by late afternoon if the clouds didn't roll in off the bay. Since the derecho six months earlier, the weather patterns stabilized. Warm mornings gave way to hot and dry afternoons filled with the occasional shower or light rainfall. The chill of fall came and went as the sun set as the buildings released their heat. Drake asked for iced coffee after Tina placed her order for a demi-breva café.

"What did you order?" Drake asked, smoothing his napkin on his lap.

"A demi-breva café. It's a half-iced and half-hot coffee with sweetened condensed milk stirred in. I don't need to add sugar. I can drink it on the run." Tina smiled as she raised her water glass. "Here's to our first solo date."

Drake coughed and sputtered as he sipped his water. Tina tilted her head, putting on her best wide-eyed stare while biting the inside of her bottom lip. Crap, her insecurities were running rampant today. Maybe with food and coffee in her, her control would return. Then there was last night's second dream and the idiot sounding like Mrs. Daniels when she berated her. Thank god the dream stopped when she turned over. That was when Jon and Drake had entered her dreams.

"Sorry, lost in my thoughts." Drake raised his water glass. "Yes, our first solo date. Here's to many more dates and the three of us together."

Tina sat her glass down. She leaned forward, cupping her chin in her hand, and sighed. Drake kept looking away and acted like he snuck a glance over the top of his sunglasses. He kept the act up until she snickered. "Drake, you're silly," she added, trying to keep from laughing harder as he took off his sunglasses and winked at her.

"Trying to break the ice. I'm still on autopilot even with ten hours of sleep. This project I'm working on has taken more creative energy than I realized." Drake stretched and laced his fingers together as he raised his arms over his head.

Tina swallowed and didn't bother hiding her reaction as his shirt pulled tight against his chest and abdomen. Six-pack abs and tight pecs were nice, but a man who looked good in a tight shirt regardless was eye candy worth devouring. Her gaze roved over Drake and back to the table.

As she looked down, her smile grew. In front of her, steam rolled off her breakfast platter. A fluffy, thick omelet, stuffed with sausage, bacon, and ham, filled one half of the platter. The other half held hash browns seasoned with cilantro and diced chunks of Mexican cheese. Next to the hash browns, two slices of thick sourdough toast cut in half lay with a small dish of whipped butter between them.

Drake picked up his coffee mug and saluted her. "Food smells fantastic. This steak looks tender enough to cut with my butter knife."

"Yes, the steak is that tender. Tilly pounds them and tenderizes each one to ensure quality and seasoning. Enjoy!" Tina picked up her fork and cut into her eggs. More steam rolled out as the interior of the omelet spilled out onto her plate. Taking a forkful, she inhaled the rich aroma and scents of the Latino spices Tilly's husband used as he cooked. The pungent tart odor of cilantro mixed with the spices he used making his own Chorizo. She saluted Drake with her fork and bit into the spicy goodness. Her taste buds popped as the heat rolled over them and across her tongue as she chewed. Three mouthfuls later, she reached for her demi-breva café. She sipped as she watched Drake cut off another portion of his steak.

His gaze met hers. He vigorously nodded. He swallowed, wiped his mouth and pointing at the steak he commented. "I haven't used the steak knife yet. That meat is fantastic. It's tangy with a hint of heat. The eggs are fluffy like your omelet. Good food."

Tina smiled as she sipped more of her café. She enjoyed good food and didn't mind paying for it. Tilly and Hector frequented the coffee shop on their way to work most mornings. The pastry shop they purchased their breads and rolls from sat two doors down the street. Tina's odd friendship with Tilly and Hector started out of business and continued beyond that. Tina set her cup down and wiped her mouth. "Tilly will appreciate the compliment. Here she comes."

A robust, tall woman with carrot-colored hair strolled toward the table. Tina smiled and waved. Tilly's smiled grew as she approached the table. "Well, about time you showed up. Hector threatened to shake his meat clever at Frank if he didn't give you a day off soon."

Tina rose and found herself enveloped in a huge bear hug. Tilly's laughter jostled Tina as she hugged her back. Scraping of chairs sounded near them. Tina stepped back to find Drake on his feet, holding his hand out, and grinning.

"Tilly, thank you for the scrumptious breakfast." Drake pointed to his half-eaten meal. "Damn fine cooking and a great cup of coffee."

Tilly grabbed his offered hand and pumped it up and down. "Thanks. Hector will be out shortly. He said he wanted a better look at the new man Tina brought with her."

Tina caught her lip between her teeth and looked down. She didn't know whether to bust out laughing or blush. Maybe both. Tilly and Hector looked after her like family. The idiot hadn't survived Hector's wrath the night he broke off with Tina. The fool thought he could come down to the restaurant and make a move on Tilly's daughter. Hector had quietly offered the dumbass two options, leave quietly, or meet up with Bertha and Mutt, their Doberman Pinchers. Neither liked the man. Two growls served to reinforce their disdain for the idiot.

"Tilly, please," Tina began, sitting back down. "I appreciate your concern. Drake is a friend of Rodger's. Janet's fiancé."

"Just the same," a bulky South American-accented voice spoke behind Tilly. "I want to meet Drake. He knows good taste in women and food."

Drake sidestepped Tilly and took Hector's hand. "Yes, I have excellent taste in food and women. I'm enjoying both today and plan to enjoy a lot more of the same."

Tilly and Hector stood conversing with Tina and Drake for several more moments as they finished eating. Hector waved before taking off for the kitchen. Tilly reached down, retrieved the check the server placed between Tina and Drake. "Finish up. This one's on Hector and me. Also, stop by the register on your way out. There's a box of cinnamon buns for each of you to take home."

Drake pushed back from the table. "I hadn't expected that. Do you think Tilly will get upset if I leave a hefty tip for the server?"

Tina chortled. "No! That's their grandson Jorge. If there wasn't a tip, Tilly would chastise Jorge for giving, to quote her, piss poor service."

Drake chuckled as he laid a five and four singles on the table. "I'll be sure to thank him for the service in front of Tilly."

Tina snorted. "Just don't embarrass him. I'm his godmother after all."

Chapter Fourteen

Drake held the door open for Tina. She carried two bags in each hand. One held two twelve packs of Tilly's cinnamon buns. The others held fresh ground coffee beans mixed with the cinnamon Tilly used in the buns. Drake wondered if Tina knew Hector had stuffed two freezer-sized plastic bags full of his dried spices and herbs he used on Drake's steak into the last bag she picked up. Regardless, Drake learned more about Tina and the people she knew and their mutual feelings.

Drake pulled his sunglass down and reached for the bags closest to him. Tina moved her hand back. "I'm fine. Let's stick them in the car for now. We can split them up before we leave."

"Before we leave?" Drake peered over his sunglasses as he unlocked his passenger side back door.

"I need a nap or a walk after eating all that. I'm stuffed." Tina handed the first set of bags to him. He placed them on the floor and turned, ready to take the others.

"How about a walk on the beach? I've got a few hours before I need to call the office. I'm working from home today." Drake sat the other two bags on the rear seat out of the sun.

As he straightened and faced Tina, he got an eyeful. Her shirt pulled tight against her breasts as she worked her hair into a ponytail, wrapping a hairband around it. Parts of her stomach peeked out from under her shirt each time the hem raised. He caught a glimpse of her navel. The place he'd dreamt about nibbling his way down from as he fondled her clit before he lapped her into one orgasm after another. Drake slowly turned away before his desire became overly evident. He could feel eyes watching them as they were parked outside Chadwicks. No need to create problems with Tilly's daughter watching from where she sat near the window refilling salt and pepper shakers.

He startled as Tina touched him. Drake slipped his hand into hers. "Sorry. I'm lost in my thoughts from time to time. This marketing project has me focused more than I realize."

"Let's take that walk and you can tell me about it. I took a few marketing classes as part of my life coaching certification." Tina fished her sunglasses out of her purse and put them on. "I really want to know more about this."

Drake began moving toward the beachfront walkway. "Several local merchants want to increase their visibility in the community as well as their bottom line with more traffic. My agency along with our national office in San Francisco is working on a coupon booklet and ads for the various merchants that Cascade Bay Times will publish and distribute."

"Sounds like an expensive venture." Tina stopped at the edge of the entry on to the beach.

Drake looked up and down the beach. Various sections showed sunbathers and beachgoers crowding areas close to the lifeguard towers. Another section further up was staked out by local surfers. A few yards up, only runners and people walking as they exercised their dogs came into view.

Tina pointed as she spoke more. "Let's make our way down to the section closer to where the private beach begins."

"Are you sure you want to get anywhere near where Madame Barracuda might spot us?" Drake shaded his eyes as they began strolling down the asphalt walkway running between the edge of the sandy beach and the concrete sidewalk alongside Shoreline Drive.

"Mrs. Daniels wouldn't be caught on a beach in broad daylight to quote Rodger. Something to do with the pool and keeping up appearances." Tina nudged Drake as he looked at her over his sunglasses.

"Okay. Don't say I didn't warn you." Drake blew her an airborne kiss and kept walking.

Tina laughed. "This project you're working on sounds like a big item. The community is going to love it I bet."

"The agency gives back to the communities where their offices are located. Twice a year we hold seminars for local businesses on how to maximize their advertising dollars. I head up the office here in Cascade Bay on this project. In fact, I've got a question for you." Drake stopped near a bench halfway down the beach walkway. He kicked off his shoes and moved out on to the sand. "Come on, it's got to be cooler near the water."

Tina sat on the bench, removed her sandals, and buckled the straps together. Carrying them in one hand, she followed Drake down to the edge of the shoreline where low waves rolled in, lapping at their toes as they continued their stroll. Tina picked up where Drake left off. "What is your question?"

"Care to learn firsthand about advertising?" Drake pushed his sunglasses on top of his head. He reached out, wrapped his fingers around Tina's wrist, and tugged. She stumbled toward him. He caught her, keeping her from falling as he slipped an arm around her waist. "Well, do you?"

Tina's snort and stiffness didn't get past him. Had he done it? Read her body language wrong and made a stupid assed assumption? What was that joke his older brother and cousins kept telling him through his teenage dating years? Oh, yeah. Never assume anything, especially where a woman is concerned. They then wrote the word assume in huge letters on the back of the football coach's play diagram blackboard. Hardest part had been explaining to coach why "ass," the letter "u" and "me" were circled several times over. Drake swallowed the apology raising fast up his throat. *"Let Tina explain,"* his conscience urged.

"Give me a moment," Tina spat out, up righting herself. "I can't answer you with the wind knocked out of me."

Drake began to pull his arm back. He stepped aside, creating space between them. A stronger need to apologize flooded him. Crap, he wanted this to work out. Jon and he discussed what either of them could do to help Tina network into a new position. One where she didn't have to spend hours on her feet hoping tips paid off on top of her hourly wage. She didn't need someone taking care of her. How did he make her a job offer that she would see as beneficial and not come across as deciding what was best for her?

"My tongue preceded my teeth." Drake shrugged as Tina stared at him. "I've got a temporary opening that pays double minimum wage for the next three months. It may work into a temp to hire position."

"I see. And you think I could do this?" Tina moved two steps ahead of him and turned. "I've taken two classes in marketing. And one art class that I barely passed."

"Don't worry about artwork," Drake said. He continued, pointing at himself. "I thought art was the basis, too. I need someone who can take a number of miscellaneous tasks and turn them into a full-time position."

"Are you looking for an administrative assistant?" Tina moved closer as the next wave rolled toward them.

"More like an intern and admin together. You'd run proofs to clients as well as greet them when they come to the office. Our receptionist quit recently. Childcare issues and a military husband prompted changes for her." Drake held out his hand.

Tina glanced away. Drake held his breath and prayed. The position needed someone who could juggle different personalities and time constraints. Tina faced that at the coffee shop. After watching her schmooze at Janet and Rodger's party, Drake figured Tina would be a perfect fit for the job.

As Tina took his hand, her gaze met his. He could make out her uneasiness. Her palm felt clammy and damp. She'd rubbed her lips together twice and sighed. He hopped she wasn't getting ready to tell him off. Drake opened his mouth to speak.

Tina smiled and raised their joined hands. "Hold on, please. Jon offered me part-time work this morning helping him with his bookkeeping. I accepted. Can you work around the hours he'll need me?"

Drake exhaled, closed his eyes, and nodded. "I'm sure I can. Let me talk with Jon..." Drake shut up quickly as he opened his eyes. Tina's fist was coming straight for his arm. He jumped out of the way, catching her as she turned toward him on follow through. "Easy, okay?"

"I'll talk to Jon about the hours he needs me and get back to you. I'm quite capable, you know." Tina glared at him.

"I forget to turn the boss switch off. Sorry, I know you're adept enough to handle both jobs." Drake raised her hand to his lips. He blew over her knuckles before brushing his lips over them. "I wanted to check with Jon if he needed you morning or afternoon. I need to figure out what my office's peak needs are, too."

"I came across hard on you. I appreciate your offer and help. I'm so used to taking care of me that I lose sight of others helping out." Tina wet her lips before continuing. "I've gotten burnt by being too trusting before. I prefer caution to blind acceptance."

"Understood. I think most folks have had similar experiences. Some of them stronger and longer lasting than others." Drake waited until her gaze met his. "It's okay. I'll work to remember this in the future."

Drake felt and heard Tina's low sigh. She looked down. He instinctively knew her gaze lingered on their entwined hands. He mentally voiced his apology and crossed his fingers on his other hand. Superstition or not, some divine help might not hurt. Praying for an intervention would change his mouth overrunning his brain.

Tina raised her head. A small smile replaced her earlier frown. Drake inhaled slowly, thanked the heavens for their help, and exhaled. Their first solo date hadn't gone too badly. It didn't rank high either. How would she react if he leaned over and kissed her? Passionately kissed her, giving into the desire he carried with him since their brief three-way sandwich outside the garage at the party? Drake clenched and unclenched his free hand, wondering how in his thirties his hormones and reaction rivaled that of a teen. Well, maybe not a teen. Certainly someone not as seasoned as he.

"I don't know where your thoughts are," Tina began, her tone warmer than a few moments earlier. "I'm not sure I dare ask either."

Drake pointed down the walkway. "Right now I want to get out of the sun. Away from prying ears and eyes, I'd answer you right away. For now let's say, think back to Saturday night when we went to check on your car."

Tina closed her eyes, dipped her head, and fanned herself with her free hand. Drake held back his laughter. So her thoughts rivaled his. Mutual interest and desire didn't guarantee a successful outcome. They might botch things up more. Drake doubted that would happen. Staying mindful made sense. He knew a fresh fruit stand further down that offered seating out of the sun. He knew midmornings were slow, leaving the outdoor seats available. Maybe there was a chance he'd get the kiss his hormones kept fussing about. They'd have privacy to talk further.

"Down at H Street, there's a fresh fruit and juice stand. They've got benches in the shade. I love fresh juice." Drake moved so he stood beside Tina.

"Tilly gets her orange juice from them. I'd love some. I'll buy." Tina stepped forward. Drake let her get to the point where she had to tug on his hand indicating her intent.

"Okay, you buy. I get to thank you with a kiss." Drake leaned closer. Close enough he could nibble her ear and neck given the chance. Instead her fragrance tantalized him, making him want to bury his face in her neck and inhale deeply. Did she wear scented lotion or cologne? He wondered if Tina knew how she affected him. If this was her natural pheromone, lord she smelled good enough to eat. And the kind of eating he had in mind couldn't be done in polite company or public. She reminded him of red hot cinnamon drops. The kind he downed as a teen. There was a whisper of chocolate, too.

Drake swallowed hard, ready to press his lips against hers.

Chapter Fifteen

Tina pulled back, unsure how to react. Kissing Drake in public where others could see them pushed her comfort level. Her heart raced as he reached for her. He watched her like a hawk swooping down upon its prey. Did she want him to stop? To not press his lips to hers and envelop her in his embrace? Two thoughts quickly entered her mind. No and Yes. Talk about indecisive.

She thrust her free hand into her short pocket. What was bothering her? Edging her near to saying no to kissing Drake, missing out on what might be a the highpoint of her morning. Maybe her day. Two job offers, two delicious hunks after her, and a free breakfast with a beach walk finishing it off...not a bad morning. The day was starting out on a very positive vibration. Where did her uncertainty come from? A voice sounded behind her.

Tina glanced over her shoulder. No, it wasn't her idiot ex-fiancé. Even though the man sounded and looked vaguely like him. Idiots each had their own flavor. Some needed nurturing and guidance. She tried with hers and gave up. Her job on the idiot makeover gig was finished. As the nerd rode by on his bicycle, Tina closed her eyes and banished any notations the idiot's ghost attempted to write on her psyche. She was in change and the idiot was dead from here on. No more listening to his recriminations and allowing self-doubt to arise. She was worth Drake and Jon. They were worthy of her. What the three of them did was their business. Not idiots, the dragoness nor her cohorts' business.

Tina rocked back on her heels, faced Drake, and smiled. "Your offer sounds lovely. I'd say race you there. I'm still digesting breakfast. Running isn't a speed I've got at the moment."

Drake winked as he shook his head. His smile reached his eyes. Tina wondered if he hid his doubt she saw earlier as he watched her. His furled brows and quick frown told her he tried to process her reaction as well as his own emotions. Maybe this was new territory for both of them. Her response to his job offer hadn't created a positive feeling at first.

Tina took a deep breath, lifting her gaze to Drake. His eyes were lower. She smiled and pressed her lips together to hold back her laughter.

Drake wanted her. She wanted him. Wanting Jon too definitely changed things. For now, she'd concentrate on Drake.

"Uh—mm the juice offer?" Tina nudged Drake as she moved closer. "You're having second thoughts?"

"Huh?" Drake looked down at her. He squinted, arched an eye brow, and blinked rapidly as though he refocused.

Tina bit her lip again, holding back her mirth. She squinted and rocked forward on the balls of her feet. No, it couldn't be. Could it? Drake's light tan didn't cover the splotches of red creeping up his neck. Ooh, the man could blush. Tina looked away lest she comment on his embarrassment.

"Juice? You know the drink made from fresh fruit," Tina offered, hoping to draw Drake's attention back to them and off his blushing.

"Uhmm, yes I remember. Sorry, mind went elsewhere." Drake shrugged. "I get engrossed in a project and lost in my thoughts sometimes as ideas come to me."

Tina reached up, cupped Drake's face, and spoke. "I believe that is part of what you thought about. I like that I got some of that action, too."

Drake's face darkened as did his neck. Tina fought the overwhelming urge to lick her fingers and drag them downward through the air. Worrying her bottom lip with her teeth, she didn't verbalize the word her subconscious yelled, "Score!"

Drake rolled his eyes. Tina could see him swallow before he licked his lips. Drake opened his mouth to speak. Tina slid her finger inside his mouth and leaned closer, whispering, "Imagine my mouth doing that to you." She stopped, looked over her shoulder, and continued. "I bet that part of you is super tasty and very delicious."

Watching Drake at a loss for words was fun. Tina knew her offer would get challenged at another point. A challenge she intended on fulfilling. One she wouldn't mind enjoying with Jon, too.

Drake let go of her hand and pointed. Tina burst out in laughter, moving forward. Glancing behind her, she caught Drake asset watching. She wiggled her hips exaggeratedly and continued down the walkway, making her way to the juice stand two blocks up.

Drake felt his heart jump as Tina walked away. He felt heat lurch up from his groin, overflowing his cock and balls and flooding over him until he felt like his entire lower half would burst into flames. Desire certainly kicked in when he got near Tina. There was more. His thoughts and actions triggered a response that had him thinking what would Tina say or think on a subject. Hell, he even wondered what the three of them would come up with as they discussed aspects of a marketing campaign or shared the events of their day as they shared a meal or cuddled together. Drake inhaled sharply. He didn't think love clobbered someone without preamble. Apparently it had or the setup was happening.

Drake shoved his apprehensions out of his head. As soon as he thought the word "love," old relationships, good and bad, came scampering back, taunting him with feelings of inadequacy and indifference. This time he knew there was more to the emotion than physicality. Could he convince his gonads and horny id that his ego might have something to say about how things progressed?

Drake picked up his pace as he followed Tina down the walkway. If nothing else came from this date, he knew they shared a common interest in enjoying their connection. And also a desire to learn more about each other while exploring their sexual curiosity as well. Drake wiped his forehead with his hand. The heat outside might rival the temperature inside once they ignited their lust.

As he entered the patio of the juice bar, Drake paused. Tina leaned against the counter, talking animatedly with the person taking orders. In the few hours they'd spent together, he'd seen a different side of her. One that he might not have gotten to know if Nita hadn't gotten sick, Aunt Helen had relaxed her date required rule, or Janet and Rodger would have eloped sooner. Things were going better than when he planned out his dating. Usually he knew about the woman before he decided to pursue her. He'd gone with his gut this time and trusted his feelings without analyzing them. This change appeared to be working out for the good. New territory came with its share of bothersome irks and quirks. Drake knew his strengths and weaknesses. Calculating played an important part in his business decisions. With his emotions and heart, imagining outcomes didn't adhere to the same rules and formulas.

"Getting good suggestions?" Drake asked, stepping up beside Tina. He slipped his hand into hers. Loosely entwining his fingers with hers, he listened to Tina's order.

"The Cascade Rush sounds good. Pineapple juice, pear nectar, guava, and mango mixed with protein powder and fat-free yogurt, please." Tina leaned against him and squeezed his hand.

Drake smiled before he brushed his lips over her cheek. "You sure that is going to be enough. Tilly's omelet must have run through you by now."

Tina grinned, stuck out her tongue, and nudged him. "I only eat twice a day with the hours I work. So brunch and dinner are it for me. This will keep me until this evening."

Drake nodded as he studied the sign with the other juice blends and items offered. He wondered how Tina would adjust to having regular hours that permitted her time for breaks and lunch if she wanted. Another nudge pulled him from his musings. "Yes, I'm ready to order. I'll have the Orange Sunrise Smoothie. Please add a banana and two scoops of fat-free yogurt. Thanks."

Tina reached into her pocket, pulled out a twenty, and laid the bill on the counter. "I'm glad we didn't go large on those. We'd need two hours of walking to work that off."

"Nah, just plenty of hot kissing and lots of orgasms," Drake whispered as he leaned closer to Tina.

Tina's reaction said more than if she'd responded out loud. She rocked back against his arm, glanced over to where the person mixed their drinks, and back to him. Drake pressed his lips together, hoping to keep his smile at bay. Yes, reactions said and did more than words. His cock pushed against his briefs. Good thing he wasn't pressed against Tina. Their behavior might not be publicly polite if he did that.

Moments later they sat on the backside of the patio area. Another couple left as they entered. A wall separated the patio from the interior of the juice bar. Cooler in the shade, Drake slipped his sunglasses off, moving nearer to Tina. He slipped his straw into his drink and sipped. Sweetness coated his tongue and slid down his throat. Better than ice cream, except the homemade kind. He understood now why his sister gave up on store-bought ice cream and made her own. He raised his drink, saluting Tina. "Great stuff. Thanks for buying."

Tina touched her cup to his. "You're welcome. Now what about your thank you?"

Drake winked and scooted closer. He looked around the patio before placing his arm around Tina's shoulders. He pulled on her, urging her to lean against him until her breasts touched him. If they were nude, she'd be pressed on him he bet. He could feel her short fast breaths as her chest rose and fell. Angling his head, Drake reached for Tina's face with his other hand. He cupped her jaw, tangling his fingers in her hair. Their breaths mingled as he closed the distance between them until their lips met.

Warm and smooth beneath his, he traced her bottom lip with his tongue as his lips parted. A dash of peppermint greeted him from the lip balm she wore. Weaving his fingers deeper into her hair, Drake massaged and deepened their kiss.

Her tongue met his as he slipped past her lips, teasing and enticing him further in exploration. Bursts of pineapple and pear skirted over his taste buds, disappearing as Tina pressed tighter against him. Her hands lay on his leg and chest. Slowly her hands slid in opposite directions. His last coherent thought reminded him no one could see them unless they walked onto the patio. Untangling his hand from Tina's hair, Drake dragged his hand lower until he cupped her breast, rubbing his thumb over her taunt nipple. Her hand nestled between his legs, stroking his groin. Tina squirmed as he corkscrewed her nipple between his thumb and finger. Her leg lifted and draped over his, trapping her hand tight against his crotch. Drake swallowed both of their moans as their tongues mimicked what they subconsciously desired. Ready to move his hand lower, Drake bunched part of Tina's top in his hand.

Tina murmured, pushing tighter against him. Her other hand fell to his belt and began wedging her fingers between his waistband and his shirt. He bunched more of her shirt in his hand.

Auuggoooga! Auuggoooga! "Get out of the water, please. Swimming is not permitted in this area," blasted out of a megaphone.

Drake wasn't sure who startled or jumped first. He quickly moved away from Tina as she combed her hair with her fingers. Her leg still rested on his.

Drake squinted as he looked out toward the beach. The county lifeguard truck resumed its patrol.

Chapter Sixteen

Tina swallowed, wondering if the lifeguard truck hadn't sounded their horn and megaphone how far she and Drake would have gone. His kiss at the party was sedate compared to today's. Somewhere between a volcanic eruption and off the Richter scale didn't begin to describe the heat and need welling up in her. Deep inside, she knew she'd never gone as far as they came close to if...if what? With Jon and Drake, it was as if no barriers existed. Well maybe some did. She lowered her guard along with her usual restraint. Maybe...just maybe, as Aunt Nell used to say, there was a scorched tail worth risking when a good looking tom cat showed up. Tina smiled as one particular memory of Aunt Nell surfaced. Marrying her third husband, both number one and two stood up for her at the wedding. When asked why she invited them, her rancorous laughter filled the air before she responded with, "They earned their retirement. Besides, a lady likes variety." Tina inhaled, wishing Aunt Nell was around to confide in about her attraction, want, desire, and possible need for both Drake and Jon.

Tina glanced at Drake. He toyed with his cup, pulling the straw in and out of the lid lying on the table next to him. He smiled at her, shrugged, and continued toying with the empty cup. Without asking him outright about his thoughts, Tina tried to qualm her unsettled feelings. Maybe nonchalant was his way of cooling things down? Or was he waiting for her reaction? From his response to her touch and unfinished fondle, he enjoyed what she'd done. She could attempt to put two and two together without figuring out a coherent answer or she could ask him.

Tina wet her lips and spoke. "Sorry."

Drake looked up, brow furled as he squinted at her. "Sorry? For what?"

"What we did or didn't?" Tina shrugged and nodded.

Drake sat up straighter and leaned forward, crooking his finger in a come-hither mode. "If you think I'm going to apologize or accept yours for responding the way we do to each other—hell ain't froze over yet. Besides, darlin', you and I would thaw it out very easily."

Tina started to duck her head as heat rolled up her neck, creeping higher onto her cheeks. Drake reached out and cupped her chin. "No regrets, okay? Nothing wrong with enjoying mutual lust and attraction. We both know there's more than that."

Tina nodded as best she could. She glanced down, knowing that her experience waited to lurch up and pull her back down into doubt and questions. Questions she knew the answers to and fought to keep answered. She suspected part of healing included acknowledging the pain of the past. Grabbing the pain by the scruff of the neck and examining it eye-to-eye took conviction. Conviction of the heart and head in agreement. Both worked together or at least complimented what the other felt. Having two guys interested in her at the same time wasn't new, but two who openly admitted, and to each other, their desire and interest...that was very different and new.

She looked up. Drake's gaze met hers. His eyes watched her, awaiting her answer. Tina inhaled and decided her here and now got better each moment spent with Drake and Jon. Risk and not knowing laid out there somewhere like a minefield littered with unexploded booby-traps. One thing she learned hardcore from her idiot time, vulnerability primed the powder kegs of ambiguity and uncertainty. There were things she could control. The key was her reaction. For now, she refused to let herself overreact as far as Drake and Jon were concerned. She offered Drake her hand, palm up, as she spoke. "No regrets."

As Drake lowered his hand from her chin, she saw his watch. Where had the time gone? Two hours had flown by. Noon on her day off and she had accomplished more than if she'd gone through her e-mail to follow up on interviews and her latest list of job leads. She wondered how the rest of the day would turn out. She winked at Drake as he laid his hand palm down on top of hers. She nibbled the inside of her bottom lip to keep from yawning.

Drake lifted their joined hands to his lips and kissed the back of her hand. "Here's to exploring more together, yes?"

Tina nodded vigorously before covering her mouth with her other hand. She yawned twice. "Company isn't boring. Not enough sleep and hours to get things done."

Drake yawned and stretched in response. "I can relate. Let's head back to the car. I need to get back and call the office. I've enjoyed myself."

Tina reached up and, cupping Drake's head, she pulled him down to her. "I wish we could enjoy more." She rose on her tiptoes and brushed her lips over his.

Drake looped his arms around her waist, hugging her tightly to him. His muffled reply raised her temperature more. "More needs privacy. If I had the time, we'd find the spot."

Tina hugged Drake and rocked back on her heels. She stumbled backward as she found her balance. She didn't need the heat of the noonday sun to know how hot it was. She pointed to the bench a few feet away. "Let's sit while we put our shoes on."

Drake entwined his hand with Tina's. They strolled in companionable silence to the bench. As she slipped on her sandals, an idea came to Drake. He needed to talk to Jon before he presented the concept to Tina. Drake pulled on his shoes and stood. As they made their way to his car, he noticed other attractive women. The eye candy sated his curious male ego. A few smiles and nods indicated their interest.

While his more macho id smiled with confidence due to Tina's presence, Drake shook his head as he unlocked his car.

After he talked with Jon, together they would approach Tina.

Drake unlocked the car. "How about we give Tilly and Hector an eyeful?"

Tina tittered. "What you got in mind?"

"Oh, this." Drake grabbed her and tugged Tina to him. Before she could back away, he wrapped his arm around her. He traced the curve of her hip with his hand until he reached her plump fleshy ass. He cupped the cheek and leaned more fully against her. Her ear and neck were scant inches from him. How much would she squirm if he nibbled her? Taste flesh that had to substitute for what he wanted to lap and suckle—her clit.

Tina snuggled into him, sliding her arms around him. Drake felt his shirt rise. He sucked in air between his teeth as Tina worked her fingers beneath his waistband. Witch knew how to tantalize. Her hands on him pulled his focus away from his goal back to his dampened desire. Didn't sweetness know the fire she played with?

Drake clenched his teeth tighter as Tina's palms flattened against him near the top of his ass. Drake softly hissed as she pushed tighter to him, trying to get her hands deeper under the waist of his jeans. "Enough," he groaned. "We don't need indecent exposure tickets happening."

He felt and heard her breathy response. With her breasts crushed against him as well as the rest of her practically plastered to him, there was no mistaking her intent. Minx knew she got to him. His cock pulsed each time she pushed against him. Crotch to crotch they stood. He hoped his icy thoughts deflated part of the tent pole threatening to announce their activities when she stepped away.

"Yes, I can be good. I got caught up in the moment." Tina brushed her lips over his as she slipped one hand then her other off him. His shirt fell into place.

"Nothing wrong with the moment. It's where we're at." Drake pecked Tina on the cheek. "Let's talk later."

Tina nodded as she took the bags he handed her. "I've got your number. How about I call you around five?"

Drake wasn't sure how soon he'd be able to reach Jon. If they were going to pull off his plan, Drake needed time to strategize with Jon. "Tell you what, let me call you. I don't know how much time I'm gonna need to finish up the coupon page I'm working on."

Drake didn't like the dejected look on Tina's face. She looked away. Her gaze didn't meet his for quite a few moments. When she did, she ducked her head as if she tried to avoid him.

"Hey, none of that," he softly offered, cupping her chin with his hand. He turned her so he could see her eyes. "I don't know what brought this on."

Tina opened her lips to respond. Drake laid two fingers on her lips. "No need for defending yourself. I want you," he paused, placing the same two fingers between Tina's breasts closer to where he felt her heart beating and continued. "To know you're important to me. I've got you inked in for a call later on. If work wasn't calling me, you'd be on your way to pleasure and more orgasms than you could count on your fingers and toes."

He watched Tina blush. Her heart pitter-pattered twice as he scraped his knuckles across her breast, along her neck up to her jaw. She turned and kissed the side of his hand. Her eyes glistened with unshed tears. Whoever put this doubt in her deserved a swift kick in his balls. The fool didn't know what a gem he'd tarnished. "Are we good?" He needed to know where they stood.

"Yes, we're good. I'm tired. Three days of double shifts is catching up with me." Tina yawned again. Drake hoped she accepted the jobs he and Jon offered and tell Frank to work doubles on his own from now on.

"Okay, for now. I'll follow you home to make sure you get there safely." Drake looked across the street. "Pull into the parking lot there and turn around. I'll be ready to follow."

Tina nodded as she pulled her car keys out of her purse. "Thanks, I appreciate that. You're fantastic."

Drake watched her jog across the street until she reached his parents' car. Once she was inside, he let go of the breath he held. If he and Jon had any say in the way the evening turned out, Tina would lose track of the orgasms pulsing through her. And maybe they'd heal the rough edges of doubt plaguing her.

Drake opened the driver's door as Tina maneuvered the turnaround as discussed. He got in and started his car. Following her home made sense. Her safety mattered more to him than his previous dates. All of their safety ranked high with him. He cared because that was who he was. He suspected Tina set off emotions and feelings the others hadn't. Another reason his gem ranked at the top of his list.

Forty minutes later, he sat outside of the apartment complex Tina turned into. He watched her unlock the front security door. She waved before entering. He waited until the door closed securely behind her. Cascade Bay's crime rate ranked below other California beach communities. Knowing Tina was safely inside her building and that she got there all right left him with a peaceful feeling. One that he'd discuss with Jon later. For now, work demanded his attention.

Chapter Seventeen

Three hours later

Drake looked up from his monitor. The conference call went better than he anticipated. Proofs for the layouts for each coupon were on their way via e-mail, followed up by regular mail from the office to the merchants participating in the back-to-school booklet.

His stomach growled as he stretched. One of Tilly's cinnamon buns and a glass of milk as a snack would tide him over until he met Jon and Tina for dinner. That was if he could get Jon out from under the car he was working on.

Drake called on his way home only to get Jon's voice mail, twice. The usual message of unable to answer working under a car didn't give details of how long he'd be. After the second call, Drake left a message. He hadn't gone into details as he didn't know when Jon would call back. The most Drake said was double date with Tina as their date. That would probably get Jon's attention. Or so Drake thought. An hour ago, Jon sent a text saying the idea sounded intriguing. Three o'clock in the afternoon didn't leave much time for planning.

Drake stood and reached for his cell phone. The phone vibrated, chirped, and vibrated again. He glanced down at the message on the screen. A text message from Jon read, "Answer your damn phone. I'm tired of reaching your screwy voice mail."

Drake laughed as he picked up his phone. He laughed harder when he saw he'd muted the phone. He didn't remember doing that. As he scrolled through the list of missed calls, he saw Jon had called three times. No wonder he sent a text instead of trying again. Drake continued toward the kitchen, calling Jon as he did. Jon picked up on the third ring.

"Well, it's about time." Jon's tone sounded a bit off. His muffled tone and chopped up speech didn't help. Drake wondered if he was still under a car working away.

"Dude, I only get one or two words before you cut out." Drake cranked the volume up on his phone, considering putting Jon on speaker to hear him better.

"Don't put me on speaker either. I hate the echo." Jon's clarity improved.

"Then get out from under the car." Drake put a glass on the counter. He reached for the refrigerator door handle when Jon's laughter blasted his ear.

Drake held the phone away from his ear, shaking his head, and blinking. He waited until his vision cleared before finding the button to lower the volume.

"Now that you rattled me," Drake began. "Can you talk?"

"Yes," Jon replied. His voice came across clearly. "Tina's car is a mess. It's a miracle she hasn't had an accident. The black goop covering the gear box and gears took three hours to get off."

Drake swallowed hard. They'd talked about her repair costs before they parted. Drake wanted to offer to pay for them to make sure she got the best parts and not secondhand like she talked about. Keeping her safe mattered. He knew Jon agreed with him. "I'm glad we did, too. She is independent."

"And stubborn," Jon added. "Hank cut me a discount when he heard who I was ordering for. Tina helped his mother out when she was sick before she moved in with him."

"Tina's known and got a heart of gold from who those I've met that she knows." Drake explained what happened during their breakfast date.

"Sounds like we got us an angel, sir." Jon's exaggerated southern drawl and twang made Drake snort and snicker.

"We both know your education is far removed from doing voice-overs."

"Well impressions weren't my strong suit when I tried standup comedy." Jon's voice returned to his normal tone.

"Nor was my being your straight man. High school talent shows added the gong so no one pelted us with rotten tomatoes." Drake laughed as Jon groaned.

"Don't remind me. Back to topic. What's this double date thing?"

"One last item before I explain. Our angel is one hot kisser and knows how to make out." Drake paused, waiting for Jon's reaction.

"Look, Hyacinth is still in the office. I'm at the counter waiting for Hank to show up with my order. So keep it clean." Jon's emphasis on clean had Drake biting his lip to keep from howling with laughter. He could see Jon trying to hide behind the small front counter and not appear as though he was adjusting his pants thanks to his cock trying to escape.

"Tina. You and me. Dinner with her." Drake kept it as clean as he could without letting his imagination run rampant. He drank part of the milk he'd poured. Even with the air conditioning on, there were no mistakes about the chemistry Tina set off.

"I think there's more to this. Hank just pulled up. You got my yes. Call you back in a bit." Jon's muffled "bye" followed by a distant "Hi, Hank" closed the conversation.

Drake ended the call. He laid his cell on the counter. He reached for the larger of the two cinnamon buns on the plate next to the glass of milk. Talk about emotional eating. He didn't care. Jacking off twice would relieve nothing compared to feeling Tina's warm flesh wrapped around him and a condom. Keeping them both safe and healthy mattered. Jon had a say in things. For now, getting them together in a safe space and relaxed topped Drake's action list. Shit, was he planning again?

Drake slid the second bun back into the box and in the refrigerator along with the carton of milk. As he drained his glass, he nodded. Planning needed caution. His tendency to over plan and analyze seemed out of place. Tina's kiss and touch set off emotions and reactions he'd felt before. Milder with other women and intense with others. This time...both pulsed over him faster than he could register his mental state. What was it his grandmother had said about falling in love?

Drake grinned as he recalled his grandmother's advice. Her British accent and southern charm added to her ladylike pronouncement. "Love is like being shot at. Except, there's no ducking or retreat. It grabs you, dousing you to the bone. You're never the same once it happens."

Oh, Tina had grabbed him, dousing him with desire, want, and an aching need. The shots continued right straight into his heart. Taking care of and looking after her pulled him away from his staunch line of taking things slow and easy. The problem remained of how he curbed his urge to fix and help. Was there an in-between?

Drake rinsed his glass and put it in the dishwasher. If Jon and he decided on dinner in, what would they fix? He hadn't had time to run to the grocery since the coupon booklet campaign started. His usually full cupboard looked essentially bare. The freezer yielded no better. A bag of meatballs and a jar of minced garlic spread didn't make a meal. Not even a nourishing snack. He laughed as he opened the silverware drawer looking for his grocery pad. A lone container of breath mints rattled against the drawer front. There was the answer to the garlic aftertaste and breath.

Yet, the answer was in front of him. A communal potluck dinner, each of them brought something to share. Jon could pick up a baguette and desert on his way over. Tina could bring the salad and pasta. That left him with a couple of jars of sauce and a good bottle or two of wine to pick up. As he scribed on the pad, making his list, he inventoried his other cabinets. He shook his head more as he opened the tall door to his pantry off his laundry room. Three cans of soup, a box of rice, and a half-empty bottle of cooking sherry greeted him. Wow, what a first impression that would make. A bachelor, limited cooking skills, and—well, for sure not a lush. He hoped he could find his cork screw and wine glasses. Eating out sounded unromantic and very planned.

As Drake reached for his reusable grocery bags, his cell phone vibrated the counter as it rang. He counted rings as he ran to the living room to find his shoes. His car keys sat on his desk with his wallet. By the third ring, he was back in the kitchen answering the phone. Caller ID showed Jon.

"Hey, that was quick," Drake answered a bit out of breath.

"Yea, Hank had two more stops to make. My order was light." Jon's next words muffled. Drake made out "Hyacinth" and "help." Then silence followed.

Drake put the phone on speaker and dropped into a chair to put his shoes on. "Damn knots."

"Damn what?" Jon's voice boomed out the phone.

Drake chortled. "Sorry, trying to get my laces unknotted. I'm about to run to the grocery."

"Well tell me about your idea first."

"How about a potluck dinner here? We each bring something. Eating out is impersonal. Besides, I think we need to talk about us." Drake finished tying both shoes, stood, stuffed his wallet in his back pocket, and sat back down.

"Us meaning you, me and Tina, right?" Jon's voice trailed off. Drake knew he waited for clarification.

"Yes, us three. Our bromance is safe. No sexual interest." Drake glanced at the clock on the back kitchen wall near his stove. Quarter to four. The run to the market would take an hour unless rush hour traffic had started. He still needed to call Tina and get her buy in as well.

"Hmm," Jon thrummed through the phone. "Have you talked to Tina? I'm game."

"About to when you called. I'd like to keep the evening to open where it goes if you're cool with that." Drake stood, cramming his list in his front jeans pocket. Either way he needed to get food in the house.

"Call me back when you're in the car. I'll conference Tina in for a three way." Drake bit his lip hard to keep from calling Jon on his innuendo. Instead he agreed and ended the conversation.

Ten minutes later he dialed Jon back. "Okay, en route. Get Tina on the line. If I'm cussing when you get back to me, traffic is a mess."

Drake clicked on his Bluetooth headset. The next stoplight, he turned on the car's hands free cell phone connection. Two loud horn blasts echoed over the headset microphone as Jon came back on the line with Tina. "Damn, dumb ass. Blowing horns won't move traffic any faster."

Jon's laugh mixed with Tina's. "Let me guess," she began. "You're on Whittier Narrows near Turner Drive."

Jon continued where Tina left off. "Stuck behind the lanes trying to merge to turn on to Main Street near the shopping plaza. Work zone still in place."

"Yes, how astute of you both." Drake hit the power windows button, closing them. He adjusted the air conditioning temperature so his teeth didn't chatter. "Can you hear me better now?"

Tina and Jon's yeses boomed Drake's ear. He tuned the volume down before he continued. "How about a potluck dinner tonight? My place. I bring the wine and spaghetti sauce."

Tina's laughter reached him first before she answered. "I think we need more than sauced sauce. I'm in if I can bring pasta and a tossed salad."

"Jon?" Drake asked, finally making the left turn he'd waited ten minutes to make. "You in?"

"Sure am. I'll bring desert and what else do we need?" Jon's voice muffled as Drake answered.

"Grab one of French Alley's small baguette loafs. I've got garlic spread to go on it. Maybe some of their gelato spumoni for desert." Drake pulled into the parking lot of McNairs Shopping Center and parked. With Tina and Jon's approval, he hung up. Dinner would be fun. Dinner discussions would be different for sure. As for the end of the evening, well that was wide open to possibilities.

Chapter Eighteen

Tina towel-dried her hair after toweling the rest of her body dry. Two showers in one day felt fabulous. Her water bill would eek up a bit for it. She didn't care. Frank owed her two checks. With those plus the pay Drake and Jon offered, she could luxuriate some. As she reapplied her makeup, Tina thought about what she might wear.

Tempting as it was to dress provocatively, she knew herself well enough to leave room for changes. Her favorite denim skirt with the slits on each side with the sandals she wore earlier made sense. Cool and light if her outdoor thermometer read right. Eighty-seven out and the breeze off the bay was waning.

That left her top choice between a print tank or a polo shirt. Showing cleavage sexied things up, getting crumbs down there didn't. She pulled on red thong panties along with a matching demi bra. Before she put on her top, she dabbed perfume behind each ear. Alluring and demure the label read. Scents of daffodils and roses mixed around her as she slid the stopper to the crystal bottle down each side of her throat until she reached the top of her cleavage. Here she plunged the stopper between her breasts and pulled it out. Flirty and sensual came to mind as she glanced in the mirror. She grinned as she caught sight of her hair. Standing up in places, flat in others, she looked like she rolled out of bed. Then again Jon and Drake might find that appealing. Pressing her legs together, she corked her perfume decanter. Enough with the sexual inferences. She needed to stop by the Italian grocer near her for fresh-made pasta. Her stomach growled, urging her to dress faster.

Fifteen minutes later, she slung her purse over her shoulder, grabbed her car keys, and strode toward her front door. The tri-colored polo shirt showed off her curves in ways she hadn't noticed before. The stripes ran from top to bottom giving her the illusion of length and drawing looks away from her bust, which filled the shirt nicely. She laughed as she stopped to admire herself in the mirror near the front hall closet. Her skirt came to her knees. The slits revealed bits of her thighs as she walked. Nothing risqué. Yet, flirty enough to attract attention. She paused as she reached for the last button on the shirt's placket. Did she close it? What if she left it open and allowed more of her cleavage to show than she would otherwise?

Tina waited until she was in her car before she made her decision. One button wouldn't make a difference to anyone except her. Because she knew about the change. Comfort and sensibility made sense. If the evening progressed in a sexual direction, she wanted to be ready. A stop at the drug store near the Italian grocer would take care of that. Condoms, male and female, along with a small bottle of lube and KY jelly rounded out the list of purchases she needed to make.

Traffic vied for access to the small shopping plaza, stranding Tina in the left hand turn lane for ten minutes before she parked. Her first stop was the grocer. Arrigo greeted her as she entered the shop.

"Bella Tina," Arrigo sang out in his deep voice. His accent remained regardless of the years he spent living in the States. He wiped his hands on the towel closest to him. He wore his hair cropped close to his head. A small, gold post earring adorned one ear. His brown eyes glowed as he approached the counter. His mustache and goatee added a rugged air to him. Tina knew it hid the clef in his chin. His wife Veronica teased him about keeping the ladies at bay with his chin covered. Truth was Arrigo had eyes for one woman, his wife.

"Why I no see you for long time?" Arrigo asked, holding his arms out as he came around the counter.

Tina stepped into Arrigo's embrace, returning the hug. "Because Frank works me hours you're open. How's Veronica and the baby?"

"She is fine. The bambino...well he is not so little anymore. Four years old and demands to be called a big boy. Antonio can be a handful for his mama and me."

Tina smiled as Arrigo kissed her cheek. "I'll have to come by on my next day off to visit with her."

"Va bene. I know she will like. What you need today?"

"Enough fresh pasta to feed three people. And some fresh grated parmesan cheese, too." Tina started toward the rear of the store. "I need salad fixings, too."

"Antipasto and feta cheese on your left in the cold case. Lettuce and other fresh ingredients in the opposite aisle. I got a nice fresh Balsamic dressing if you like." Arrigo moved back behind the counter toward the kitchen area where he made pasta.

Tina glanced at her watch as she gathered the ingredients for the salad she planned to make. Drake's place, according to the address he texted her, would take forty minutes to reach in rush hour. She hoped traffic had thinned out by the time she got finished at the drug store.

Twenty minutes later, she was back in her car after promising Arrigo she'd call Veronica next week. The drug store stop took no more than five minutes as she was one of five customers in the store. As she turned on to Lakeshore Drive, Tina clicked on the radio to her favorite classical music station and settled back to enjoy the shore and beach scenery as she drove.

Drake pulled the bottle of red wine he bought earlier out of the refrigerator. Three turns of the cork screw and a soft pop filled his kitchen. He set the bottle on the counter to let it breathe and warm a bit. Wine glasses, utensils, napkins, and plates sat next to the bottle. There wasn't more he could do until Jon and Tina arrived.

Jon phoned as he left the shop. Their brief discussion bemused Drake. Desire topped their topics. Neither one denied their attraction and wanted to take things further. The last time they tried a threesome, the woman dumped both of them a week later. The sex turned out awesomely hot and steamy. They'd fallen asleep blissed out. Turned out the woman had her sights set on another friend of theirs. She later admitted to using them to make the guy jealous. Things resulted in a broken friendship and two bruised egos. Jon agreed with him that making sure everyone understood each other before lust took over made sense.

Drake knew he wanted more than a temporary fling. He didn't know about long term. More than a passionate make out session determined that. Heck, more than hot steamy sex determined that. What he learned from seeing Tina interact with others combined with what he knew about her overall personality and her connections with people in general pointed to a good potential for the long term. Her connection with Jon figured into this, too. Tonight might be about feeling each out and not in a physical sense. He wasn't ruling out what might or might not happen. He hoped Jon arrived early so they could talk more.

Drake glanced at his watch. He had thirty minutes to grab a shower and change his clothes. As he trotted toward his bedroom, Drake started humming. A song from his youth came to mind. He didn't have time to clap his hands. He knew he was happy. Maybe this was a sign of the evening to come.

Jon gritted his teeth and stuck his head under the cold water pouring out of his shower. The water temperature would even out soon. This happened when he turned the faucet halfway on and stepped in the tub without checking the water temperature first. As he soaped and rinsed, Jon puzzled over Drake's last comment before he hung up.

Drake mentioned cohesion and unity. And not forgetting the Debbie incident. Jon lathered his hair as he recalled what happened with Debbie. He closed his eyes, ducking his head back under the lukewarm spray.

Debbie's lithe figure and riotous blonde curls flashed before him. Her aquamarine eyes glowed when she smiled. He had noticed her confidence and poise from across the room the first time they met. Even Drake had found her charm and flirtatious manner attracting. Most people at the party knew each other in some fashion. Debbie's circles of connection touched practically everyone present. By the time, the night was over, both he and Drake had Debbie's number. Somewhere in between their third and fourth get-togethers over the ensuing weeks, Debbie cornered them separately, refusing to take no for an answer. The results turned out disastrous. Casual sex turned her on until their buddy Clyde showed an intense interest in her. Then Miss Ice Queen appeared.

Jon shook his head as he moved out from under the shower. From what he'd observed watching Tina and getting to know her over the past six months, she and Debbie were nowhere close in comparison. Still, he understood Drake's reservations. Talking before pursuing did make sense.

Fifteen minutes later, Jon finished tying his sneakers and took a final look in the mirror. His worn Doobie Brothers reunion t-shirt aged him. He didn't care. Tonight was going to be laidback and easygoing. He picked up his wallet off the dresser, looked inside, smiled, and stuffed it in his back jeans pocket. Inside two foil condom packets rubbed against each other. Prepared and ready.

As he pulled out his apartment complex parking structure, Jon clicked on the radio. Smooth jazz poured out the speakers. He cracked open all the windows and worked his way down to Lakeshore Drive. The thirty minute commute to Drake's was underway.

Drake turned off his blow-dryer as his doorbell rang. He slid his bare feet back into his deck shoes. He snagged his clean black polo shirt off the bed, pulling it on as he made his way down the hall toward his living room. He inhaled as he passed the kitchen doorway. Spices, essences of tomato and garlic greeted him. In the background, a hint of cherries, pears, white pepper, and tart apples lingered. His stomach growled as he entered the living room. He hoped Jon and Tina were hungry, too. His grandmother's basic pasta sauce recipe and meatballs simmered in the crock pot sitting on the counter.

Two more rings later, Drake opened the door. Jon thrust a double handled paper bag at him as he entered. French Alley's logo stood out on the side. Drake took the bag, peering inside.

A white plastic bag stood out against the brown paper wrapped around the warm baguette. The white bag held a half-gallon container of spumoni gelato. Next to the white bag and behind the bread, two bottles of seltzer rattled. Drake turned, reaching for the door, when Tina came into view.

"I'm on time, right?" She grasped the doorknob, pulling the door closed behind her as she entered. In her free hand, she held a bag bearing the local Italian market's logo.

Drake could make out the butcher paper holding the fresh pasta Arrigo made. Other items deeper in the sack caused it to bulge. As if on cue, his stomach growled louder than the last time. Jon smiled and snickered. Tina burst out laughing. Drake looked down at his stomach and scolded. "Quiet you. You'll get fed."

Chapter Nineteen

Drake poured wine and seltzer over cracked ice as he refilled each glass a third full. Dinner had gone wonderfully so far. Tina and Jon both bounced questions off him concerning the local merchants and their possible concerns with the upcoming coupon booklet release. Now with their dinner plates soaking in the sink, Tina sat out the cheese and crackers she brought with her at Arrigo's insistence. The man's pasta accented the sauce and meatballs deliciously.

"I bet the spaghetti noodles had extra parmesan in them. The tang had to be from dried tomatoes." Jon picked his wine glass up off the counter and sipped before continuing. "The onion and dried garlic added a zing to your salad, Tina."

Drake watched Tina duck her head and nod. She had a shy side? He wouldn't have thought so. There were things to find out about each other and a discussion to begin.

"Tina," Drake began, sitting down with his wine glass in hand. "Is it hard for you to take a compliment?"

Even though he couldn't see more than the side of her face, Drake didn't miss the way her lips pressed together. Great, had he set off a chain reaction?

Tina rinsed her hands and wiped them on the towel she used to take garlic bread out of the oven. She picked up her wine glass and sipped before making her way to the table. As she sat, he studied her, waiting to see if her body language gave him any hint of what was going on in her mind.

Tina picked up a piece of cheese, nibbled a bit of it, and sipped more wine. She cleared her throat and spoke. "Some compliments I'm used to. Others no. Having two guys interested in me at once—well that is new."

Drake leaned forward, reaching for Tina's hand. He took a hold of it as he spoke. "Darlin', I appreciate what you're saying. Jon and I did this once before. It's not exactly passé for us either."

Jon cleared his throat as he turned his chair sideways. Drake knew from that angle Jon could see Tina and him. Drake leaned back. "Jon, speak up."

Jon nodded and reached for a pitted olive. He bit into it, sending juice squirting out. Tina grabbed a napkin and shoved three more at Jon while Drake stood up. Jon coughed, gulped wine, and spoke. "Sorry. I'm not sure where to begin except I don't want to repeat past mistakes."

Drake walked over to his home office that took up one corner of his kitchen. He opened a drawer, pulled out three pens. Then he opened one of the upper cabinets and pulled out a legal-sized tablet. He moved back to the table handing Jon and Tina each a pen and three sheets of paper each. Drake sat down and tore three sheets off the pad for himself. He nibbled a cracker and piece of cheese while he gathered his thoughts. After a couple swallows of wine, he spoke.

"I think we've got fears and concerns happening. Can we write down our top three and share them with each other?" Drake picked up his pen and pulled one sheet to him. "I'll go first, okay?"

Tina and Jon nodded as they picked up their pens and a sheet of paper each.

Drake glanced down at the paper. He wrote a numerical one and paused. What concerned him most? Getting things right? Being certain everyone was on board? Or was he still carrying trepidations from the Debbie incident?

He thought a bit longer and wrote as he spoke. "My number one item is uncertainty. Debbie burned me good. I'd fallen hard for her."

"Debbie?" Tina asked, reaching for more cheese and crackers.

"Yes, Debbie," Jon confirmed, touching Tina's arm. "Our joint relationship with her backfired." He explained briefly what happened before writing his number one concern down. "My number one is clarity. Too much got left unsaid. Important things weren't discussed."

Tina picked up her pen as she reached for her paper, she spoke. "Competition. The last two guys I dated decided to see who could outdo the other. What a mess. Then there's my failed engagement."

Drake stood up and moved around the table. He touched Jon's shoulder, nodding as he eased around him. Jon rose, too, following in Drake's wake. They both reached Tina at the same time. Drake eased the pen out of her hand. Jon took a hold of her arm. They slid their arms around her together enveloping her between them as they hugged her tightly. Each kissed her cheek.

Jon spoke first. "Drake and I aren't in competition. We don't need to prove ourselves."

"I agree," Drake confirmed. "Some guys think everything needs competitiveness. Relationships and sex don't work that way."

Tina smiled as they stepped back. "I don't need other women to compete with either."

Drake made his way back to his chair. He drank more wine and picked up his pen. "There's a word for what we're attempting. I found it today researching different lifestyle choices. The word is polyamory."

"Polyamory?" Jon asked, arching an eyebrow as he spoke. Drake could see the questions running through his mind. Jon loved crossword puzzles and the more advanced the better.

"Yes. It's being romantically involved with more than one person at the same time." Drake printed the word in capital letters on a blank sheet. He pushed the paper to the center of the table.

Tina pulled the paper to her. Drake watched as she read the word. She looked up, glanced from him to Jon and back. Her shoulders slumped forward, more relaxed than he believed. She held her head at an angle that hid part of her face. Was she having second thoughts? Anxious now that the three of them were discussing their intent and interest?

Drake reached for Tina's hand as she pushed the paper back to the center of the table. Her gaze met his and looked away. He glanced at their hands, noting hers laid over his as she reached for Jon. Drake reminded himself to breathe. He bit the inside of his bottom lip, afraid if he spoke he'd stop the scene happening in front of him. This wasn't an illusion.

Drake looked up as Jon took Tina's hand. A smile grew as Jon began nodding. Drake glanced back to Tina. Her eyes locked with his. Her smile deepened, reaching her cheeks that started flushing and igniting a glow in her eyes.

Drake swallowed hard. His pulse throbbed with excitement each time her thumb rubbed the underside of his wrist. Christ, if she affected him like this now, what would the evening bring?

Jon cleared his throat, drawing Drake out of his thoughts, back to the three of them. "We've got two more things to go, right?"

Drake nodded. "Why don't you go next, Jon?"

Jon heaved a sigh, picked up his pen, and wrote as he spoke. "My second concern is truth and the third is decency. I need to know we're upfront with each other and treating each other with respect and civility."

"I can relate. Especially after Debbie and a few others I dated. What about you, Tina?" Drake turned in his chair so he could see her.

"My second is casualness which leads to my third, desire. I'm not looking for a fling or an affair. I desire and want something more." Tina shrugged and continued. "I guess it's too early to know what this is."

Drake squeezed Tina's hand. "Since we're here talking about this, I believe the potential for more is on the table."

Jon untangled his hand from Tina's. He laid his hand, palm up, on the table. "I'm here because I want to be. Drake and I agreed the next woman who struck both our fancies simultaneously we would take our time with."

Drake chortled. Tina and Jon looked at him with puzzled expressions. Jon's arched eyebrow almost copied Tina's. Drake held up his free hand as he spoke. "No offense. Jon's and my discussion took place more than two years ago. We're not vulturizing you."

Jon snorted and joined Drake's banter. "Yes, like Snoopy in the Charlie Brown comic." He arched both brows, sucked in his cheeks, and opened his eyes very wide while glaring at Tina.

Tina clapped her hand over her mouth, muffling her meeps of laughter. She started laughing harder as Jon stuck his thumbs in his ears and wiggled his fingers. All three broke out in loud laughter.

Five minutes later, Drake wiped his eyes. "Oh goodness. I haven't laughed that hard in a while. Thanks, Jon. Levity is good for you."

Jon rose, bowed, and raised his glass. "Here's to us. Here's to what comes, who we'll be, and the journey."

Tina raised her glass, touched Jon's, and faced Drake.

His glass remained on the table. His hand caressed the side. "Before I raise my glass, I want to voice my number two and three."

Jon and Tina practically responded in unison. "Yes, please do."

Drake stood with his glass raised. "Here's to us. And to genuine interest and honesty."

Tina rose and clinked her glass with his. She faced Jon. "I'm interested. I desire both of you. And I'm enjoying our time together."

Drake moved around the table until he stood next to Tina. He motioned Jon to come up on Tina's other side. As Jon approached, Drake intertwined his arm with Tina's so their glasses were side by side. Jon entwined his arm so all three glasses were together. Drake cleared his throat. "Here's to a start, a beginning, and us as a trio."

Glasses touched. Wine slid down their throats. Quiet filled the kitchen as they stood cuddling together. The tick of the wall clock faded into the background as Drake carefully withdrew his arm. He set his glass on the table. He reached for Jon's and Tina's. Moments later, their hands free, Drake slid his arm around Tina, pulling her to him.

"Darling, we started something this morning. Also, the night outside the garage. Shall we continue?" Drake leaned in, nuzzling Tina's neck. He nipped and worried the flesh covering her jugular. As he worked his way up to her ear, he cupped her breast. Her fullness filled his hand nicely, allowing his thumb and forefinger to touch her nipple.

Jon's arm laid on his. Drake could feel the change in Tina's breathing. Her short burst of warm air blew over his cheek. Drake raised his head and caught Jon watching him. His coconspirator winked at him before Jon lowered his head to the back of Tina's neck. Drake didn't need to see Jon's movements to know where and when he cuddled up to Tina. Her sharp intake and moan said it all. Jon's hand moved up between them, cupping Tina's opposite breast.

Jon's muffled voice reached Drake as he began sucking Tina's earlobe between his lips. "Delicious after dinner dessert."

Drake caught Tina's flesh between his teeth as he smiled. More breathy sighs and moans greeted him. The evening was young and pleasure awaited them.

Chapter Twenty

Tina tried to focus on more than Drake's caresses and Jon's whispers of what he wanted to do next. One of her hands rested on Drake's shoulder. Her other hand occasionally touched Jon's hip and thigh as he moved back and forth against her. Heat didn't begin to describe the feelings careening through her.

Cool, then shivering tendrils of need worked their way over the areas exposed as Drake worked his way along her jaw, nipping and soothing with his tongue as he went. Jon's breath lingered along the sensitive area near the base of her neck before his movements sent air across the locks of hair standing up as if begging for more of his touch. The moment both touched her, it was as though they worked in unison. She knew they might have discussed their tactics prior to getting together. Yet, each seemed to be working independent of the other.

Tina swallowed hard and gave into the urge welling up in her. Raising her hand, she stroked upward along Drake's cheek until she touched his hair. She threaded her fingers into the locks closest to her. As her fist closed, she reached backward with her other hand until she touched Jon on his next move tighter to her. His cock, hard and pushing against his zipper, brushed over her questing fingers. She cupped her hand and reached lower. His next pass practically placed him, balls and cock, in the palm of her hand. She tugged softly with her hair-filled hand and squeezed gently with the other.

"Ouch," Drake remarked. "That smarts." He looked up, his eyes meeting hers. The glow in his eyes grew as she tugged again.

"Got your attention, do I?" Tina licked her lips, fighting against leaning into kiss him.

Jon's muffled sigh wrapped around her, alerting her to his enjoyment. Jon's lips pressed against her neck, close to the baseline near her left ear. He licked then blew on the wet spot he left. Need slammed into her, taking her deep into the pool of molten want ready to escape her volcanic interior.

Tina cupped Jon firmer in her hand and squeezed again. This time she pressed upward with her hand, tightening his cock and balls to him. Another shallow moan escaped him as he nipped her earlobe.

Drake shook his head, drawing her gaze back to him. He smiled, licked his lips, and blew a kiss to her. Tina gulped air as her lips parted. Swallowing, she reminded herself to breath. Her nipples pebbled as thoughts rushed through her. One image refused to fade. Jon between her legs licking her into one orgasm after another as Drake penetrated her vaginally.

Drake bunched more of Tina's top in his hand. Heat rolled off her in bursts he hadn't felt since Debbie. He knew this time this wasn't about getting someone else jealous or catching their attention. This was about him, Jon and him in particular. Placing his palm flat on Tina's stomach, he felt and heard her sharp intake of air. He smiled and moved closer.

Jon came into sight as Drake stood mere inches from Tina. Flushed cheeks and rumpled hair greeted him. There was no mistaking the desire flooding him. His eyes shined with that knowing smile Drake knew and understood. Last time he'd seen that smile was with Debbie. And Tina was *not* Debbie.

Drake inhaled as Tina did. He slid his hand up her stomach, delighting in her murmurs and small gasps. Warmth gave way to heat as he cupped the underside of her breast. In between breaths, he could feel the staccato beats of her heart. There was no mistaking how turned on she was.

"Nice ass," Jon murmured as he swayed from away from Drake's sight. "Plump and firm."

Tina jerked forward, almost plastering herself against Drake. Drake ground against her, easing his fingers under her bra. As he angled his head, Jon swayed back into view, his eyes glazed even more. Drake winked and leaned in, pressing his lips to Tina's.

A loud thump and crash echoed through the kitchen, jolting the trio apart. Drake shook his head, turning from where the sound came from. He rushed toward the back door muttering. "Damn raccoons!"

He flicked on the outside light as he opened the door, two sets of glowing yellow eyes blinked at him. He started to raise his hand as he opened the screen door. Soft mews began, followed by barks from the yard next door. Drake stepped out onto the porch. His eyes adjusted to the dark as he moved closer to the garbage cans laying on their side. Two calico cats scrambled into view. "It's Mrs. McGiddy's cats," he called out.

Jon came into sight as Drake looked over his shoulder. "Is she out of town again?" he asked, stepping onto the porch.

"Must be. Rusty is carrying on barking. I best check what's going on." Drake moved past Jon and back into the kitchen.

As he got near Tina, he quickly kissed her on the cheek. "Sorry for the interruption. I need your help."

Tina smiled as she pulled down her top. "Sure. What can I do?"

"In the front closet is a pet carrier. Grab it for me while I get my keys. We've got a cat to corral."

Tina's snort set him to grinning. Jon's high-pitched "Here, kitty kitty" echoed through kitchen. Drake drew in two deep breathes and a quick exhale to keep from laughing as he trotted down the hall toward his bedroom.

Tina held the carrier out to him as Drake made his way back through the living room. "Thanks, now comes the fun part. Getting these two pesky felines in here."

Drake took the carrier and started into the kitchen as Jon called out. "Look out, inbound cat." The slam of the backdoor closing followed.

Two blurs of calico color rushed by Drake and disappeared under his couch. Drake jumped back into the living room mere seconds before Jon barreled past him.

"Hey," Tina called out, grabbing Jon's arm as he approached the couch. "Slow down. Get some of the ham from the antipasto plate. Rinse it off. I'll entice them out from under the couch."

Jon nodded as Tina dropped to her hands and knees in front of the couch. Drake bit his lip again. Talk about pent up angst and hormones kicking. Taking Tina from behind while she sucked Jon off might reduce the lust contorting his groin into convoluted knots. Sucking in air through his nose, Drake pushed his horny ego and id aside as he moved around the back of the couch.

Tina's hand shot up in the air as she looked up. She began gesturing at the couch. "Put the carrier down here. We can put them in after we catch them."

Drake nodded, placing the carrier with its door open on the couch. "How are we going to keep them from getting out?"

Tina smiled as she shook her head. "You sit next to it and keep ready to shut the door. Jon can help me get the rascals out."

"Hey, Jon," Drake called, making his way around the couch. "Come help Tina."

Jon appeared in the living room, his hands out in front of him holding two pieces of ham dripping water as he moved. "What ya need?"

"First go dry the meat. Second, help Tina corral Willow and Bella." Drake dropped onto the couch, pulling his feet up as he sat. He scrunched down next to the carrier. He turned it so the door swung close to his outside hand near the front of the cushions. He stretched his leg out behind the carrier, ready to stabilize it as two cats got stuffed. The latch that locked the carrier closed stuck out, ready for the push needed to ensure the two felines didn't make good on their escape attempt.

Jon re-entered the living room. He carried the ham in one hand. In his other, he had two dish towels. "The stench of those two as they ran past—well you may want these, too, when you get them." He tossed the towels to Tina.

"Willow and Bella?" she asked, catching the towels midair.

"Good catch," Jon replied. "Yes, Mrs. McGiddy is a paranormal fan. Said the cats reminded her of her two fave characters."

Drake shrugged as Tina glanced to him. "I don't ask. I just occasionally transport them to the vet for her on her way out of town."

Ten more minutes passed before two yowling cats clamoring inside the carrier made their way back toward their owner's home with Drake, Jon, and Tina accompanying them. Another twenty passed chatting with Mrs. McGiddy and reassuring her none of them were worse for the wear from tending to Willow and Bella.

Back inside Drake's, Jon dropped into the chair next to the couch. "What a way to end a date!"

Tina laughed, perching on the arm of the chair he occupied. She ruffled his hair. "Who says the date or evening is over?"

Drake picked up a towel and rubbed down the cushions. "Very little cat hair. Good." He tossed the towel on the end table next to him. "Yes, who said anything about over?"

Jon shrugged. "Well, the mood sure changed."

Tina kissed his cheek, stood, and offered him her hand. "I need a hug. A Drake and Jon hug." She held out her other hand to Drake.

Both men rose, encircling Tina. Jon reached down to adjust his crotch. His cock stayed swollen during the cat rescue. Watching Tina's pert ass sway under her skirt as she walked along with the feminine bounce of her breasts did little to cool his want and lust. He practically creamed rubbing against her. He ached to sink balls deep into her and soak while he stroked her clit until she cried out in multiple orgasms, riding him until he reached a huge, ball-tightening climax himself. Would any of them get off tonight? He needed, too. Did Drake and Tina second his hunger?

Drake nudged him as he got close. He rolled his eyes and adjusted his waistband, making a fanning motion with his hand. Jon nodded his agreement. He hoped Drake understood. Jon moved closer to Tina.

Tina held up her arms as Jon and Drake got closer. Jon slid his left arm around Tina's waist, cuddling her into his side. Drake mimicked his move on her right side, snuggling up to her. Jon motioned Drake toward him until the three formed a circle. Jon cleared his throat, looked at Tina and Drake, and spoke. "Before we go farther, I need clarity."

Tina cuddled tighter to him. "Sure, Jon. What will help you achieve this?"

Drake bobbed his head in agreement. "Right, Jon. What Tina said. We're in this together."

"Do we want to make love or just fool around?" Jon glanced to the floor, gritting his teeth against the answer he hoped wasn't coming.

Tina's sigh reached him first. Her head lolled on his shoulder as she spoke. "I'm open to both. I've come to know both of you over the six months Janet and Rodger dated. Even more personally since the wedding plans and arrangements."

Drake started speaking as Jon looked up. "Bro, a long time ago I made up my mind that I could fool around. But..." Drake held up his hand as Jon opened his mouth to retort. Drake continued, preventing Jon from speaking. "I'm a lover first and foremost. I care for both of you."

Jon grabbed Drake's wrist, tugging it down. "I'm falling for Tina, too. I ain't asking for a lifetime commitment tonight."

"Why not?" Tina tossed out.

Jon pulled away from Drake and Tina. His mouth dropped open as he shook his head. He glanced at Drake who stood gapped mouthed staring at Tina, too.

Chapter Twenty-One

"Well, why not?" Tina asked again. "I mean after all none of us are kids."

Drake stuttered as he walked toward the couch, dropping onto it. "I–I'm not sure."

Tina nodded as she faced Jon. "Your reason?"

Jon opened and closed his mouth, shrugging as he did. He clenched his hands a couple of times before holding his hands up in front of him and backing away.

Tina struggled against the overwhelming urge to wrap her arms tight around herself and leave. Leave to where? Grabbing her purse and fleeing wasn't going to fix the question stymieing everyone. No, she'd grown beyond doubting herself. Janet and the people of Cascade Bay had helped with that. Even Tina's parents were right about being true to herself. She was worth more than any of her failed relationships and far richer since her failed engagement. If she wanted Jon *and* Drake, communicating this mattered as well as talking about why she popped the question she had.

She licked her lips, rubbed them together, and turned. She walked the couch, leaned on it, and spoke. "Are we moving too fast? I get the feeling that I spoke out of turn."

Drake stretched his legs out so his feet lay on his coffee table. His arm lay along the back of the couch placing his hand near Tina's arm. She glanced to see where he looked. His eyes were on her. He smiled. He scowled for a moment then quickly nodded. He raised his hand pointing with one finger toward her.

"I've planned and overanalyzed past relationships. Did the same with ones that went pretty well. Caught me off guard is my best answer." He toed off his shoes and drew his knees up to him. He sat up, hugging his knees as he continued. "We've known each other a fair amount of time. How deep have our conversations gone?"

Jon burst out laughing. Tina and Drake glared at him. He made his way to the couch, perching on the arm opposite Drake. "Sorry, nerves. I've dated a few outspoken women. Most of them were so headstrong that partner wasn't in their vocabulary."

"And your point is?" Drake asked, leaning back as his arms slackened their hold on his legs.

"If this is going to work, partnerships are important, right?" Jon sat down on the cushion close to him.

Drake opened his mouth to reply. Tina cut him off. "We've each talked about our number one concerns. Uncertainty, competition, and clarity."

Jon and Drake both nodded.

Tina continued her train of thought. "Well, you told me you aren't in competition."

Both nodded again.

She held up two fingers. "We've stated our certain desire and interest."

Another set of nods followed.

"Okay, then we're clear on wanting to move forward, right?" Tina gritted her teeth, hoping that someone other than she spoke up this time. She resisted the prod from her past to rattle on. Prattling more wouldn't do any good.

Tina focused on Jon. His prior moves and actions spoke volumes of his hesitation. She understood that her stomach refused to stop flip-flopping along with her sweaty palms. Her nerves were telling her how scared they were.

She leaned forward more until she rested on her elbows intently watching Jon. It was almost a stare down. His eyes met hers. The room around her faded until...

"What the—" Tina called out as a cold hand wrapped around her forearm. She looked down, ready to pull away. Drake's hand came into view. She glanced to her left, catching his sheepish smile.

"Sorry," he offered. "Now that I got both of your attentions."

Jon and Tina smiled as they nodded.

"Enough with the bobble head moves," Drake scolded, joining their laughter. "Tina's right. We've talked and commented on our main issues. I think the others got covered, too."

Jon held up a hand as he nodded. "I'm agreeing," he quickly added. "I value both of you. I don't want to lose either. Is that clear enough?"

Drake exaggeratedly bobbed his head up and down before he swung his feet off the couch. As he turned his head to check on Tina, he caught Jon sticking his tongue out at him.

"Dude," Drake fussed, pointing at Jon. "I ain't French kissing you. So put your tongue back—"

"I am," Tina dared and caught Jon's face between her hands. She leaned over to him and pressed her lips to his.

"—in your mouth," Drake finished, watching a smoldering kiss unfold before him.

Jon's hand came up to Tina's shoulder. Her hand visible to Drake worked its way through Jon's hair, leaving patches standing up as she threaded her fingers deeper into his locks.

Drake twitched as his view moved downward. The outline of Tina's taut nipple pushed against her top. There was no mistaking how turned on she was. Drake reminded himself to breathe and enjoy the simmer. There were benefits to voyeurism, especially during a scalding hot threesome. Additional benefits came from the warm-up which he intended to be a part of. Compersion also became relevant. Appreciating Jon and Tina enjoying each other fueled other things and added more enjoyment for him and the three of them.

Drake glanced up to find Tina and Jon watching him. Drake jerked and shuddered a bit. "Stop that," he retorted. "Not nice staring at me like that."

Jon smirked. "And you weren't busy taking in the view?"

Drake stuck his tongue out. Jon began shaking his head as Tina spoke. "I'm taking advantage of this."

Her head with lips puckered blocked Drake's view of Jon. Not that Drake cared at the moment. He leaned forward, his own lips puckered, ready for Tina's kiss.

Her lips met his. He reached up to steady her as she leaned toward him. Her hand slid up his arm until it rested on his shoulder. Working his fingers into her loose locks of hair, he kneaded gently, urging warmth into his touch. His free hand moved upward until her breast, taut nipple and all, filled his palm. He traced her areola with his thumb, close to her nipple and back down the underside toward her ribs.

Tina opened her mouth as her subtle spasms reached his hand. Drake closed his eyes and pressed his lips firmer against hers. He traced the small opening of her lips with the tip of his tongue, waiting for a signal she was ready for an age old mating dance to begin. He'd tasted her earlier on the beach as tart juice flavors from their smoothies mixed, tantalizing each of them with the headiness more passion could add. Now the sharp cheese essence mixed with the cracked pepper crackers they'd eaten as they talked after dinner. Her tongue met his as he ventured deeper into her recesses. She gave as good as she got. Their tongues dueled, chasing and retreating until they broke apart gasping for air.

"Wow," Jon huffed. Drake looked down to where Jon's hands rested close to his crotch. The telltale sign of his turned-on state bulged against his jeans' zipper. Drake knew the ache and want that echoed what Jon must be feeling. They needed, Tina included, follow through.

Drake cleared his throat and spoke. "I agree we're all on the same page. Maybe the next question is are we looking for exclusivity or long-term right now?"

Drake reached up and caressed Tina's cheek. "Babe, why don't you sit between us? Makes conversation easier without needing to crane my neck to see Jon."

Tina made her way around the couch, stepping over Jon's legs so she stood in the space between the couch and the coffee table. She smoothed her skirt and sat.

Jon sighed as she settled between them. "I think we're too new to decide either. Though I think focusing on us makes sense."

Tina picked up Jon's hand and voiced her thoughts. "I agree with Jon. Let's focus on us for now. Maybe we can check in periodically to see where we're at to realign as needed?"

Drake entwined his fingers with Tina's free hand. "I feel you're both correct. I got a need to make you come and cream in your pretty mouth." Drake raised Tina's hand to his lips, licking her fingers and slowly mimicking what he wanted her to do to him orally.

Tina gulped, squirmed, and glanced at both. Jon's smile and wink told her of his interest in similar pursuits. "You two know how to make a lady feel wanted." She raised their hands to her, brushing her lips over each of their knuckles.

Drake stood, cussing as he bumped into the coffee table. Jon tried to shove the table out of the way as Drake tried to help Tina stand. "Ouch," Jon hissed through clenched teeth. "Those corners are sharp." He shook his hand.

"You all right?" Tina asked, turning Jon's hand over.

"Yes," Jon responded.

Drake didn't bother repressing the grin that curled his lips. Tina opened Jon's hand and kissed the redness crossing his palm. They needed more room if they were going to get anywhere tonight. Instead he faced Jon and Tina, offering each a hand. "We need more room. I know the place."

Once Tina stood, Drake let go of her hand. Jon shook his head and rose on his own. "Are you talking about your man cave?"

Drake chuckled. "Yes, my spacious bedroom complete with a California king-size bed. Pillow top mattress included."

Tina glanced from Jon to Drake. How did Jon know so much about Drake's bedroom? She held her retort and question. The two of them were best friends. They spent enough time together they were bound to know specifics about their respective places.

Jon's next statement confirmed her suspicions. "Helping each other move and pick-uping purchases."

"And house sitting," Drake added, stepping into the hall.

Tina moved around the couch and bent down to retrieve her purse. Her purchases rattled against the small plastic bag inside. Forethought appeared to be paying off. As she up righted, she found Drake and Jon ogling her. "What? Do I have a couple of ass men on my hands?" Tina blushed as Drake began nodding rapidly followed by Jon's. She held her purse aloft. "I came prepared."

Jon's lopsided grin caught Drake off guard. He turned so neither could see his face. Time for true confessions would come soon enough. Threesomes could be interesting for sure. While neither he nor Jon was sexually interested in the other, they enjoyed aspects of bend-over boyfriend play with the right woman shared between them.

He looked back over his shoulder at Tina who grinned and moved toward him. Over her shoulder he could see Jon bringing up the rear, nodding vigorously.

Down the hall, past the kitchen, Tina looked in the first open door Drake moved past. A small second bedroom appeared. Blues and teals filled the room. A double bed, small chest of drawers dresser, and nightstand were all she could see. The full length mirror on the closet door she caught a glimpse of reflected a small, full bathroom through another open door. The next door down, Drake stopped. He waited until Jon and she caught up to him. He smiled and bowed. "Welcome to my man cave."

Drake strode into his bedroom. Tina followed him. Her mouth dropped open as she entered. Rich mahogany wood grains greeted her. The mauve and deep burgundy accents offset the deep beige-cream colored walls. In the far corner, a large overstuffed wingback chair, a floor lamp, and an end table filled the space. Books, two deep in three piles, covered the table. As she moved further into the room, Tina closed her mouth as the poster bed came into view. A thick crocheted afghan lay across the deep, rich burgundy comforter covering the bed. Huge plump pillows decorated the head of the bed intermixed with smaller lighter shades of the same color with bits of mauve here and there. "Wow," was all she could say.

Chapter Twenty-Two

Tina faced Drake and Jon. Both men had pulled their shirts off. Jon was seated on the bed, removing his sneakers and socks. Drake walked to his closet and hung his belt inside. He moved back to the bed, sat on the cushioned-topped hope chest near the foot of the bed. He sat with his legs spread apart, crooking his finger at her in a come-hither motion.

Tina moved toward Drake. Her throat went dry as she took in the sight before her. Drake's chest hair matched that on his head almost perfectly. The inverted V trailed downward, disappearing into his jeans. Jon's chest appeared smooth and pale in comparison. She didn't care. Both were too delish to worry about comparing when the contrasts suited her just as well. The subtle highlights running through Drake's locks, she bet, were natural given his tanned physique. Jon's six-pack abs rippled as he rose. Neither man had an ounce of flab if anyone asked her. They were going to bolt when she got naked. The thirty pounds she lost since working for Frank showed with the creases and stretch marks marring her belly. Her breasts sagged, no longer perky like in her twenties. Tina stopped dead, a few feet from Drake. She looked down, swallowing hard, fighting back the tears threatening to start. So much for confidence.

Jon leaned down, stuffed his socks in his shoes, and tossed them near the wall out of his pathway to Tina. He rose, noticing her downward glance and non-movement. Drake sat still. Jon glanced to Drake, seeing if he was paying attention or signaling him. Nothing. Jon inhaled, pondering what to do next. Tina seemed unsure and confused. Heck, he didn't blame her. They were in Drake's bedroom shucking clothes and she still stood in front of Drake holding her purse like a prized possession. Some reassurance might help.

He strode toward her, talking as he went. "I helped pick out the colors for each room. Drake did the same with my place."

Tina looked up as he spoke and moved toward her. Jon continued his banter. "We chose the colors to match our rooms at home. I love teals and blues. They remind me of the beach and the view from my balcony."

Drake chimed in. "Yes, I've always loved the woods and the sun rising and setting over them. That influenced my choices."

Jon exhaled as Drake held out his hand to Tina. Maybe the road bump was small. She glanced at Drake and back to Jon. Jon's throat constricted. A single tear ran down her cheek. He knew of one way to help, a hug and then another hug. Actions spoke louder than words his parents taught him. He chose to let his actions speak for him.

Jon closed the distance between him and Tina quickly. He made sure to stay within view. No need to startle her and create more problems. He slid his arm around her, pulling her close, speaking as he did. "Darlin', talking about what's eating at you can help." He squeezed her to him, let go, and repeated.

Drake stood, closing the space as well. "No one is going to move faster than anyone wants." He cupped Tina's face and tilted her head back until they were eye to eye. Jon watched and waited.

Tina sniffled and talked. "You're hunks. Both of you. I'm..." Her voice trailed off. Jon side hugged her again.

Drake took her purse, setting it on the hope chest seat. He turned back and retook her hand. "You're beautiful."

Tina opened her mouth to retort. Drake quickly placed two fingers against her lips, shushing her. "I don't care what others told you. I see all of you. Inside and out. I know what beautiful is for me."

Jon moved around Tina, taking her other hand. She glanced at him. He waited until her gaze fully met his. "I find you delicious. Utterly awesome. Fascinating and very attractive. To echo Drake, I know what is beautiful for me. It's you."

Drake spoke again. "We've gotten to see parts of you over the last two days that some wouldn't get to know. Six months ago we started becoming friends. Now we're about to become lovers and more."

Jon could feel Tina's eyes back on him. He nodded, kissing the back of her hand as he did. "What Drake said, I echo again. And add this, let us show you what we mean."

He almost missed Tina's slight nod. Her eyes darted back and forth from him to Drake with each agitated breath she took. Jon wanted to envelop her in a bear hug and hold her until she cried herself out. God, what moron had dented this woman's self-worth so badly that she doubted her own inner beauty and didn't realize how that caused her inner loveliness to sizzle and shine. Jon shook his hand behind him, fighting against fisting his hand as he pictured what he would like to do to the fool. No, that solved nothing. The solution came in showing Tina how beautiful she was in their eyes. It would take time to heal the doubt. Time he was willing to take, and he bet Drake was willing to take, too.

Drake lifted Tina's right arm. He looked to Jon. Jon didn't need words to understand what came next. He captured Tina's left hand in his, raising her arm as well. Drake reached between them and took hold of the hem of her shirt. Jon copied Drake's move. Both men started raising Tina's shirt at the same time. They continued until they were right below her breasts.

Drake flattened part of his hand on her. He could feel the rapid pitter-patter of her heart. She broke eye contact with him long enough to gaze at Jon. She seemed to watch each of them for some sign or look. She didn't fight them on leaving her arms up. Drake let go of Tina's arm and bunched more of her top in his free hand. Jon did the same after he kissed her cheek. Drake caught part of his whispered words. Jon knew about reassurance and quietly letting the person know they were all right. His work with Holt and Torrey at Ladies Satisfaction Shelter gave him the experience he needed.

Tina ducked her head as Drake and Jon worked her shirt higher. Belief in herself ran deep on many levels. Recovering from three bad relationships in a row left damage she wasn't aware of. Time for healing had come. She bent at the waist, letting them pull the shirt over her head and off her. She reached up and pulled the scrunchie from her hair, shaking her head to free it. Her locks flowed over her shoulders, tickling them as she moved. She smiled as Drake threaded his hands deeper into her hair as he kissed her cheek.

Jon took her scrunchie, tossing it on top of the hope chest. The glow in his eyes grew the closer he got. Tina didn't think her nipples could get any harder or her breasts more swollen with longing to the point of aching for both men to touch her.

Touches as though they read braille began along her ribs, extending with each stroke up to her shoulders and back to the underside of each breast. Tina didn't know where one action started and another stopped. Both men's hands felt like heaven on her. A warm stroke, a whispered endearment, and broad chests that held her between them like the crème filling in a cookie brought her to a blistering boil and back to a simmer as Drake stepped away.

He reached for the comforter, his regard never leaving her. It was as though he and she were the only ones in the room and yet Jon remained connected to her. His arms loosely encircled her waist, pulling her back until she lay flesh to flesh with him. Breaks in their contact occurred due to the clothing separating them. Drake smiled as Jon cupped first one breast, then her other. Weighing them with his palms as if he considered their size and perfection, ripe melons ready for consumption. Capturing each nipple between his thumb and fingers, he plucked and rubbed while pressing tighter to her.

Drake pulled the comforter to the foot of the bed, bringing with it the top sheet. His next movements recaptured Tina's attention. He reached for the waistband of his jeans, unbuttoning them. Next, he unzipped the zipper partway, flashed a pair of blue briefs he wore underneath, and zipped the zipper closed. His hips began swaying and rocking to a song only he could hear. Dancing, he made his way back to where she and Jon stood. Feet from her he halted before turning around. What seemed like an eternity passed with each breath she took. His hips continued shimmying with a rocking motion imitating the act of intimacy. Every breath Tina took pressed her fuller against Jon. There was no mistaking his status either.

Jon nipped her shoulder, marking her and igniting a part of her she didn't understand. There was a claiming happening at a primitive level. One of the men honored her with his mark, his sign of possession. The other had yet to claim her. She knew before the night was over there would be no error as to who and what they were. More than friends, not yet fully lovers, and a deeper commitment perhaps to come.

Jon rubbed against her, nestling his cock at the edge of the cleft of her ass. Each time Drake rocked his hips back in his dance, Jon rocked forward, pressing tightly to her, letting her know the depth of his desire. Jon leaned forward, whispering hot in her ear. "I'm so wet. Dripping wet, wanting to bury my cock balls-deep in you. How wet are you?"

Every pull and tug on her highly sensitized nipples shot streams of hot liquid need deep into her. Her clit throbbed in a counter rhythm to Drake's dance, wanting him to possess her. Jon's bites and caresses pushed her closer to the edge. She'd had a nipple orgasm with her idiot fiancé. The act stimulated and scared her then. Could she relax and let the pleasure she wanted happen this time?

Jon's breath warmed her ear as he suckled a lobe into his mouth. He worried the tender flesh with his teeth, nipping lightly as he tweaked first one nipple then the other. His hips and crotch rocked against her in a counter rhythm that brought her tight to the edge. The edge of orgasm pulsed through her, tossing wave after crest, followed by another growing in intensity until she raised her arms, thrusting her breasts fuller into Jon's hands. Rocking back against him, she let go a deep pent-up sigh and rode the backsplash of the heated wave of need tumbling her higher to a crescendo of release unlike her prior experience.

Her nipples ached and tingled, echoing the constriction of her clit as another surge of relief tossed her higher into the heights of orgasmic delight. She could feel her breasts swell, straining against the cups of her bra as though the material couldn't contain them. Each sweep of ecstasy washed her toward the whirlpool of gratification she sought.

Jon gave in to the smile of satisfaction claiming him. Lusciousness filled his hands. Feminine flesh rolled over him and pushed back on him as he brought Tina to another peak and crest of release. Each time she swayed back to him, she pressed harder against him. Jon stiffened his posture, ensuring both of their safety. He wanted Tina, focused on her pleasure and trusting him to keep her safe. Trust didn't happen easily. He understood her precautions. After Debbie, it had taken him and Drake a while to recover. Jon suspected the same held true for Tina. Maybe together, the three of them could help each other.

Chapter Twenty-Three

Drake stopped dancing, his hands reaching for the waist of his jeans again. Watching Tina respond to Jon turned him on immensely. His cock nudged the zipper of his jeans, letting him know his arousal grew as Tina bent forward as she pushed against Jon. Her apparent arousal showed from her half-closed glassy eyes, the outline of her firm nipples tenting her bra cup, and the savory noises emanating from her. Jon's reaction came through loud and clear as well. He rocked to her as she pressed against him. His eyes mimicked hers in many ways. There was his grin that grew into the masculine smile that said his ego hummed with pleasure as he pleased his woman. Drake chuckled to himself as he shucked his jeans. As he looked down to ensure he stepped clear of the pile of clothing at his feet, he couldn't help but notice the growing wet spot near the fly of his briefs. Pre-cum leaked over him, leaving telltale signs of his arousal.

"Yes," Tina moaned, her voice laced with pleasure and arousal. Drake knew that tone from their earlier bout of passion. Her arousal reached out to him, enticing him to join Jon and her.

Drake kicked his jeans aside and moved around the bed. As he reached Tina, her hands reached out to him. Her lopsided grin combined with her puckered lips left no doubt to her intent. She wanted him. Drake closed the distance between them, clasping Tina's outstretched hand.

"I'm here, babe," he murmured, slipping his arm around Tina's waist, drawing her tighter to him.

Tina closed her eyes as she inhaled. Pressed against Jon, heat flowed between them, buffered by their clothing. Exquisite torture didn't become either of them. Her breasts ached, straining and pushing her bra until it pulled tighter across her. Her thong panties wedged deeper into the cleft of her ass cheeks to the point of working her damp wetness back and forth over her engorged clit.

Drake's arm slipped around her waist, urging her forward to him. Coolness swept in, filling the air as she separated from Jon. Wisps of chill curled up under her skirt, bringing brief relief to her scalding mons. Passion savored in small nips and nibbles didn't compare with the headlong dive deep into its embrace. She knew pacing and timing mattered. Neither Drake nor Jon was going to rush her. She didn't want to rush them either.

Tina glanced over her shoulder to capture Jon's look before she snuggled into Drake's embrace. Jon's wink before she turned away blew out any lingering anxiety and concern. His hands were moving downward. She could only guess his destination.

Drake's chest loomed before her like a pillow inviting her head to lay on it. She stroked her hand up and down the skin before her. Warmth combined with muscles rippled beneath her palm. Sounds rumbled under the flesh that led her gaze upward until her eyes met Drake's observation. His smile reached his eyes, illuminating his face in a megawatt way that spoke of his want and hunger. His lips parted as he cupped her chin. Tina leaned in to meet Drake. His hand tangled in her hair as his lips covered hers.

If smoke were a by-product of the steam rolling off Drake and Tina, Jon would need a fan to see them. He unbuttoned his jeans. They rode low on his hips as he loosened his belt. There was no missing the growing wet spot on Drake's briefs before he pulled Tina to him. Jon wondered if his spot took up the same space. Heat flowed off each of them, pooling around them only to encircle again before rising to engulf them.

Low sounds of pleasure escaped their lips. Jon smiled, nodding and unzipping his jeans. Kicking free of them, he shoved them next to his shoes and T-shirt. His gaze remained fixed on Drake and Tina. Drake's free hand reached around Tina, sliding along the back of her bra in a to-and-fro motion. Jon squinted, looked closer. He caught his upper lip between his teeth to keep from laughing. Apparently Tina wore a front clasp bra. The clasp held well. She hadn't fallen out of it yet nor had the clasp sprung like some other girls he dated had.

Jon reached for the zipper of Tina's skirt as she turned. She shook her head, sending her hair tossing like a short whip. Part of it smacked his arms. The sting didn't stop him. He worked the two buttons holding the waistband closed while he opened the zipper. Soon Tina stood before him clad only in her thong panties and bra. If she kept moving, her feet would get caught up in the skirt pooling around her ankles.

Jon rubbed his hands up Tina's back until he reached her shoulders. He noticed the tense muscles that tightened under his touch. Was she aware of her reactions? This could be a result of Drake's caresses.

Jon began to kneel. He pressed kisses along the path his lips followed. He nipped above and below the waistband of Tina's panties before moving lower. He rubbed and marveled at the firmness of her leg muscles. He knew the long hours she worked contributed to this. Would she enjoy a massage? Another way to ease them into full nudity and relaxing on the bed? For the moment, Jon lifted one foot, then her other, pulling her skirt away from her feet. He eased each sandal off her feet.

"Thank you, Jon," Tina said, her voice coming from over his head. Jon looked up. Drake and Tina peered down at him. Both grinning like Cheshire cats. Jon arched his eyebrows, rolled his eyes, and...

"Jon!" Tina gasped, reaching for her left buttock cheek, closest to Jon.

Drake laughed, shaking his finger at Jon. "Hungry? Or wanting seconds?" Drake asked.

Jon pointed to himself, shook his head, and grinned. "Just letting you know I'm here."

Tina chortled. "You sure did."

Jon rose, hooked his thumbs in the waistband of his briefs, and started to shuck them. "I'm hot, bothered, and horny."

He skimmed his underwear down his hips, stopping short of pulling them completely off.

He glanced to Tina, whose eyes glowed with mirth and eagerness. Next to Drake, whose stance sent Jon into peals of laughter. Drake stood with one side of his briefs pushed midway down his hip. His waistband bunched around his abs, acting as a buffer between him and Tina. Jon pointed at Drake, chuckling. "Dude, I think we're at similar stages."

Drake leaned back, bobbed his head up and down, then back and forth, exaggerating his movements prior to answering. "I do believe you're right," he said in his best Sherlock Holmes voice.

Tina snorted and turned so Jon and Drake could clearly see her. Jon noted where the cups of her bra bunched, exposing part of her breast. Drake's efforts to undo her bra clasp showed some success. Jon stood, walked over, and stopped in front of Drake. Jon bowed, pointed to Tina, and reached out, touching the area where Tina's bra bunched the most.

"This is our culprit," Jon said. He took ahold of one side of the middle of the material, pulling it slightly off Tina's breasts. Part of her light pink areolas came into view.

Jon grasped one side of Tina's bra with his left hand and the other with his right. He moved his hands up and down unfastening the center clasp of Tina's bra. As he stepped back, her lush full breasts came into view.

Tina fought the urge to fumble with her bra. Strong feelings coursed over her. Sexy and alluring came through, chased away by self-doubt and worry, and last by far the strongest ones washed over her, certainty and awareness. Certainty she wanted to be here. Awareness things were on a new level.

Jon thrust his briefs off his hips. They fell to the floor covering his ankles and feet. He stepped free of them. Drake moved to where Tina could easily see him take off his briefs.

Two gorgeous hunks of maleness stood before her. Drake's inverted V of chest hair ended at his waist. As Tina's eyes roved lower, there was no mistaking Drake's darker shades of brown matched the color nesting his cock and balls. His arousal jetted out, proud and erect, announcing his salacious interest. She could make out a sparse covering of hair on his balls as he stood legs apart. Her eyes flitted to Jon. His light colored down halted at his waist, restarting at the apex of his legs in a deeper blond that nested his cock and balls. His cock poked through his thatch. It too announced his prudent want and need. Tina knew size didn't matter if the owner knew how to use their cock and techniques in bringing and giving pleasure. Neither Jon nor Drake lacked in size or shape. Drake appeared a bit more endowed than Jon. So far each of their styles had her scrumptiously turned on and ready to sample more.

Jon reached for one of her shoulders. Drake reached for her other one. Each, with a bra strap in their fingers, eased the straps off her shoulders, down her arms, and off her. Tina tossed her head, working her hair off her shoulders and down her back. She stood before them clad in her wet panties. She could feel their looks move over her. Drake nodded, wetting his lips. Jon reached for her. He hooked his fingers in the waist of her panties, tugging them downward.

Tina looked down. Her panties hung around her knees. The darker portion of them glistened with her orgasmic fluids. She closed her eyes, feeling her cheeks warm slightly. A hand enfolded hers. She opened her eyes to find Drake putting her hand on his shoulder. His soft smile and brief thumbs-up gesture with his free hand reached into her, cupping her heart in a broth of warmth that pooled and overflowed, cascading over her.

"Let me help you with those," Drake offered. He leaned down and tugged, sending her panties down her legs and on to the floor. They, like the guys' briefs had, settled around her ankles.

"And I'll assist here," Jon continued, squatting next to her. He lifted one foot, then her other until he held her panties in his hand. He tossed them on top of her discarded skirt. Jon stroked his hand upward along her ankle onto her calf, reaching higher upward toward her thigh. Tina squeezed her legs together.

"I need to clean up a bit," she claimed, squeezing harder as Jon trailed his fingers over her pubic hair. "Taste gets enhanced with a bit of soap and water."

Jon looked up at her, smiling and licking his lips. Tina swallowed hard as she caught Drake smiling and nodding, too. She could hear the chime of Drake's clock in the living room. By the time Jon rose and started toward Drake's bathroom, she counted nine chimes. The evening faded into night without her realizing it. Under the cover of night, they would venture into new territory together. Somewhere in the ensuing hours they passed from unsure, uneasy, and doubtful to ready, willing, and able. They had more to cover and work through. That could wait. Focusing on here and now added depth and opportunity to build on what may come. Tina hoped her intuitions were right.

Chapter Twenty-Four

Drake took a hold of Tina's hand as he walked past her. Jon led the way into the large master bath. Drake knew when he did the remodeling, a large dual-headed shower made sense. One detached from the other creating a nozzle which made rinsing or wetting down easier for quick showers. Tonight would show how accommodating the shower was as the trio washed together.

"How do you like your water? Lukewarm or tepid?" Jon asked, sliding the door closest to him open. He reached inside and pulled out three large fluffy towels. Drake took two from Jon, tossing them on the counter separating the two sinks. He reached for the third, instead grabbing air. He looked up. Jon winked at him. Damn. Caught watching Tina's reaction in place of paying attention to what Jon did.

"Wow," Tina crooned, touching the blue and burgundy wall tiles. "The colors are awesome."

"Thanks," Drake replied. "Made sense to combine the main colors of both bedrooms into the bathrooms."

Tina nodded as she faced him. "You've got a knack for color and décor. I like."

"I appreciate your compliment." Drake combed his hands through Tina's hair. "Do you need your scrunchie to keep this off you while we shower?"

Jon reached for a drawer near them as Tina replied. "Yes, otherwise it will take most of the night to dry out. Even blow drying leaves things damp."

"There are clips in here. Remember your Mom left them last time she visited." Jon pulled two large butterfly hair clips from the drawer.

Drake and Jon helped secure Tina's hair. She stepped inside the shower and turned the water on. "I like tepid water. What about you?"

Jon moved in close to the faucet, testing the water as he did. "I like both. I'm fine with this temp."

Drake slid the other door open and entered behind Tina. He reached around her, examining the water temperature as well. "I'm good." He closed the door.

Drake closed the limited space between him and Tina. Pressed flesh to flesh, warmth increasing to heat wrapped the two of them together. Her neck lay bare before him. Easy access. Soon his lips and teeth followed their earlier path up and down her tempting neck. His pleasure mattered on hers. Mutual enjoyment plunged both into higher and hotter orgasmic bliss.

Jon's hand met his as Drake moved his hands along Tina's ribs. As Jon came into view, he held a bar of soap. Drake sniffed. His usual brand's fragrance filled his nostrils. Nothing overly masculine, not flowers either. He nodded.

"You okay with the soap?" he asked, nipping Tina's earlobe.

He felt and heard her reply. She arched against him, shivered with small rapid shudders, moaned, and responded. "Yess–ss."

"Good," Jon added, wetting the bar and lathering his hands. As he rinsed them, he added. "I'll wet down. Then Drake and I will do you."

"Right, I can get your back as I wet me down," Drake said. He held out his hand to Jon. "I'll hold the soap while you wet down."

Ten minutes passed as the detached showerhead and hose passed back and forth between Drake and Jon. Soap slicked down Jon's chest, calling Tina's hands to help with washing him. On her second pass working soap down his chest toward his waist, Jon covered her hand, guiding her lower until she touched his hard cock. He rocked forward, slicking his length with soap. His neck arched as he closed his eyes, tossing his head back, groaning his delight as she enclosed her fingers around him.

"Can't take too much or I'll come," Jon moaned.

"Savor it bro'. We need to get our lady washed," Drake offered.

Jon nodded as best he could. Tina's hand on him set off urges that threatened to flame out of control. Jon sucked in air as he curled his lips around his teeth. He clenched his hands and eased out of Tina's hand. Exhaling, he accepted the soap from Drake, lathered his hands, and reached for Tina.

First he took a hold of her wrist closest to him, working the soap up and down her arm. Next came her shoulder. Jon slowly and gently drew his soap slicked hands over her breast. Soft and plump, they rolled beneath his touch like down in a pillow. He could see himself at the end of a day cuddled to her with his head on her breast.

"Turn to me so I can finish your other half, please." Jon held up his soapy hands after washing her waist and top of her thighs. Tina faced forward to him, allowing him to complete cleansing her other half. Jon retrieved the soap from Drake and squatted. Soon his re-lathered hands worked their way up her leg, coming close to her mons. He blew on her wet hair and soaped her other leg down to her ankle. He looked up. Drake and Tina were passionately French kissing. Jon waited until they broke apart before reaching between her legs.

Tina shuddered as she inhaled. Jon's wet fingers traced the outline of her mons and dipped in to rim her clit before resuming their looping path down and across her thigh. He reached between her legs, rubbing and stroking her perineum as he made his way toward her buttocks. His nails dragged light upward along the lower underside of her ass cheeks.

Behind her Drake worked his soapy hands up across her shoulders and in long strokes down over her tired muscles finishing at her waist. She watched as he again soaped his hands. As he placed the sudsy bar in the dish, he leaned down, kissed her ear, and whispered his intent. "I feel your excitement and heat every time Jon touches you. I'm gonna ramp things up."

Two sets of strong male hands cleaned and soaped her ass. Jon caressed her lower portion, gripping and releasing to soothe and appease the muscles along her hips down to where they joined with the muscles of the backs of her thighs. Drake worked soap in smooth strokes down one side of each cheek. His strokes fondled and cupped the fleshy portion Jon's touch didn't reach

At the same time, Jon eased a finger inside her. With soft and gentle thrusts, he worked his digit in and out until she relaxed, permitting him a deeper penetration. He kept up the light pressure on her clit that kept it throbbing and pulsing with each rub. As he stroked deeper, he touched her G-spot. Tina panted with need that increased with her dual on-switches massaged repeatedly.

Drake stopped his larger circles and began making smaller, slower ones over and across her nipples, tweaking them in between strokes. His voice pulled her into the pleasure cloud swallowing her. "Relax and enjoy. I'll stop when you want me to."

Tina shook her head as Jon withdrew his fingers from her. He kept steady short strokes and pressure going over and against her swollen clit. She felt him move against her as he stood. She watched his movement through her semi-closed eyes. He pressed closer to her, speaking as he did. "Part of me was in you. Lovely response, sweetie." Jon quickly brushed his lips over hers before continuing. "Let Drake take you to the next level, please."

Tina swallowed hard. The heat of passion could blur understanding and thought if one didn't proceed carefully. She didn't want to hurt like that again. Tina held her breath, closed her eyes, and waited for her heart to speak to her. Neither Jon nor Drake had pushed her beyond her comfort when she'd hesitated up to now. Drake softened his strokes when she hadn't answered him. Some never got pleasure. Others enjoyed the act as part of their lovemaking. Tina knew attempting the act with someone she trusted and felt comfortable with might help. Trust was growing with both men. She knew them well. How well did she trust herself? One last deep breath followed by a quick exhale. Tina made up her mind.

"Yes, Drake. Slow and easy. If I say stop, halt. Okay?" Tina tensed ready for a fight against assault. Drake slipped his arm around her, pulling her tight to him. He kissed her cheek, and spoke. "Babe, no one is going to hurt you. I promise you that. Pleasure first and foremost. I agree."

She cuddled fuller against Drake. Jon completed the front half of her double male sandwich. His lips covered hers. His questing fingers found her stiff clit and reached past, coating his digits with her wetness. Heat poured over her, sandwiched between both men. Pleasure ebbed and flowed as a crest and wave of delectable bliss washed through her.

Jon pulled and plucked her nipple near him. Drake nipped and laved her neck and ear. Wanton need dripped from her core deeper into her, tightening her nipples and clit more. One pulse, then another began with one enormous thrust into rippling orgasms rushing upward with abandon splashing her. Each splash coated her with more fervent ecstasy.

A deep groan, followed by smaller moans and pants rolled out her parted lips. Tina clutched Jon's shoulder. She leaned harder on Drake as multiple orgasms rocked her. She gave herself over to the tidal wave tossing her upward toward unbridled bliss. Her eyes closed. Her breathing seemed to rush in and out in time with the pleasure coursing over and through her. Twice more she shuddered, forgoing any coherent thought or form. One last crash and toss found her breathing heavily as she opened her eyes. Jon winked at her. He slowed his strokes on her clit. Murmuring about after care, he let go of her nipple and slid his hand to her waist. He worked his arm around her, cradling her to him.

Jon caught the look on Tina's face. She was blissed out. Her mind hadn't gotten back to full throttle thinking yet. Right now all of them needed to rewash on their own and then decided where they went next.

Drake stuck his hand and the bar of soap under the shower flow before he spoke. "Wow. I need a cleanup and some of that water. Jon can you push the button for the other showerhead?"

"You bet," Jon replied. "We all could use a quick cleanup."

Tina accepted the soap from Drake before he rinsed down and exited the shower. She quickly washed. Taking the handheld shower from Jon, she rinsed down while he soaped and rinsed under the main shower. Drake opened the door closest to him while Jon turned off the showerheads and water. He held out a plush, extra-large bath sheet to her. His towel dipped around his waist like a sarong. Tina quickly wrapped up in the towel, making room for Jon to exist the shower. He quickly caught the towel Drake tossed him. Soon the three of them stood clad in towels basking in the warmth from the heat ventilating off the ceiling fan heating unit. Drake and Jon held their hands out to her.

Chapter Twenty-Five

"Let's adjourn to the bedroom," Drake proposed, slipping his hand into Tina's. "I need to catch my breath. How about you?"

Tina nodded before looking to Jon. Jon's infectious grin had Drake smiling. Jon's eyes glowed as he gazed at Tina. Drake knew the look. Jon was falling deeper for Tina. Drake kept his words inside. Each of them had crossed a threshold in the shower. One that brought them to a decision pinnacle that might make or break their newly formed connection. Drake felt his own heart reach out to Tina as she hugged Jon. Hearts didn't break. But they sure ached when things got fouled up. Debbie's perfunctory way of doing things wasn't going to happen here. Precaution and safe sex mattered.

Drake tossed his towel on the floor near his clothes. He climbed into bed and lay back on his pillows. Jon perched on the opposite side of the bed while Tina hovered in the bathroom door.

Jon pulled his towel off and dropped it near his clothes. He patted the mattress space between Drake and him. Tina's towel sagged in places. Even though she wore the towel wrap-style, she wasn't clutching part of it nor stuffing the gapping sides tighter under her arms. Jon breathed deeper. He let go of the angst he could feel creeping up on him. Whether he or Drake cared to admit it, Debbie's mark marred pieces of the evening. Experience couldn't be totally erased. He wasn't going to let Debbie's ghost hinder the evening any more. He let go a deep sigh and swung his legs up on the bed. Sitting cross-legged, Jon patted the mattress again, offering his hand to Tina. He glanced over his shoulder at Drake.

Drake leaned forward, holding out his hand. Jon caught Drake's smile before turning back toward Tina. Several moments of quiet passed before she moved. The towel slowly slid down her body revealing the feminine flesh that made up Tina. A full lush figure defined by curves. Curves that nipped and tucked in all the right places. Jon knew societal beauty brought with it a vanity he couldn't stomach. Too many vain women cared about themselves in almost a narcissistic fashion. He'd met many down-to-earth ones. Tina's inner beauty spoke to him in a way that turned him on. Her confidence enhanced the outer parts. Parts he intended on touching and pleasuring again.

Tina paused, holding her towel before her. She could feel the heat rising up and filling the room. When she looked at Drake or Jon, there was a glow that she hadn't seen for a while coming from them. Their eyes mirrored their smiles.

She felt the familiar shards of prior doubt and rejection waiting to envelop and dominate her once again.

. This time she wasn't going there. She trusted herself and knew what she wanted. She wanted the two men who sat waiting for her to make the next move. Two who pleased her, turned her on, and sought their mutual satisfaction as three. Yes, everyone was on the same page.

Tina tossed her towel on the floor next to Jon's. She pulled the clips from her hair, placing them on the nightstand near Jon. She briefly touched her lips to his, rubbing her hands up and down his chest. Pulling back, she looked over his head. Drake blew her an airborne kiss. Tina returned it. Yes, she was where she wanted to be. Another round of hot and consensual pleasure awaited her.

She sat on the mattress, pulled her feet up to her, and scooted across until she sat middle of the space between Drake and Jon. She faced both, seeing their faces, their masculine bodies, and deliciously handsome cocks hard and glistening with drops of pre-cum. Her mouth watered at the thought of tasting them. Oral sex pleasured the giver and the receiver. Bringing a man to orgasm took flair and finesse. Things she devoted to learning.

Tina slid her hands under her thighs, not sure where to put them. Her eyes darted back and forth from Jon to Drake. Each appeared to be watching her, possibly awaiting a signal. What signal she didn't know. Licking her lips, she spoke. "You look like you got something to say."

Drake turned on his side, tugging one of the pillows close to Jon into the middle of the bed. Jon added another from behind him to the group. They patted the pillows. Jon turned on his side facing Drake. Tina swallowed hard. Without words each was making their desire known. Before she gave into the lust swirling around them, she needed answers. She hoped they did, too.

Tina held up one hand. "Before we go there..." She paused, unsure how to phrase things without appearing blunt. Tact didn't always offer the best or simplest way to ask what some would consider required knowledge. Timing mattered. It needed to be now. Not after the fact.

"What about safe sex? STDs?" There, she said it. She nibbled the inside of her lower lip, awaiting the fury her questions might unleash.

Jon turned on his back, his hands behind his head. His cock stood at attention, saluting her and making its desire known. More cum leaked out as Jon spoke. "I use condoms for intercourse. No dates in a while. Last check up and tests were clean six months ago."

He reached down, ran his hand over his cockhead, and stroked downward. Tina tried to breathe. Watching a man pleasure himself turned her on. Though she'd come, being multi-orgasmic ensured her more pleasure awaited her. She rocked back on her hands before she gave into her growing need to taste Jon.

Facing Drake, she spoke, hoping to distract her hormones and escalating desire. He copied Jon's moves before he answered her.

Drake's eyes closed as he stroked to his balls and back to the top of his cock. His other hand cupped his balls. He panted briefly before he stopped, squeezing the tip of his cock as he shuddered. Opening his eyes, he smiled, licked his lips and replied. "Condoms here, too. A couple of dates here and there the last six months. Last tests clean last week. Clean checkup two months prior."

Almost in unison, Jon and Drake said, "You?"

Tina jumped, pulling her gaze away from Drake's. She inhaled quickly and sighed. "Condoms, too. Came prepared. Clean tests and checkup last month."

"Good," Jon said, rolling to his knees. He tugged on her arm, working her hand free from under her. He pulled her to him. "You catch your breath while we get things laid out."

Drake tapped her shoulder as she rolled out of Jon's embrace, catching her as she fell toward him. Drake threaded his hands into her hair, fisting bunches of it in his "The night is made for loving. You are the one I want to love the night away with."

Drake leaned toward her. His eyes locked with hers. Tina willed herself to blink. She couldn't. His eyes slid closed at the same instance hers did. Lips warm and moist brushed over hers. They pressed firmer, urging her to open to him. Tina inhaled and reached for Drake. His hands rubbed and massaged her scalp, setting off tingles of charged shivers racing downward. Down into her core, igniting the smoldering red coals waiting to combust and leap into flames of wanton desire.

Behind her the mattress dipped. Warmth covered her back and buttocks. Jon cupped her breast, rubbing his thumb over and around her stiffening nipple. His hot breath cascaded over her neck and shoulders the closer he got. As Jon's lips touched the back of her neck, Drake's tongue pressed against her lips. Tina reached down and in front of her until her hand met flesh. Hard male skin slid beneath her palm. Drake's throated moan vibrated her lips and his. Her fingers closed around him.

Reaching behind her, she brushed against Jon. His abdomen rippled under her questing fingers. His soft moan caressed her ear, warming her with his breath.

Parting her lips, Tina met Drake. Their tongues dueled as before each tasting and teasing until they pulled apart, breathlessly hot and even more bothered. Tina gulped air and squealed. Jon's chuckle heated the spot he nipped.

Shaking her head, Tina scolded him. "Play nice, Jon. Not so hard with the teeth."

Jon's arms slipped around her waist, pulling her back to him as he responded. "Sorry. You taste good."

Drake's snort drew Tina's focus forward. "Jon, you didn't get enough to eat at dinner?" Drake asked, trailing his fingers down her cheek.

"I want dessert. Crème de Tina." Jon's voice warped over her ear and down her neck, sending more tendrils of delight sparking the coals already glowing deep red inside her.

Tina swallowed, inhaled, and squirmed. Jon's short laugh rumbled her back down to her hips. His hard-on brushed against her, leaving a wet mark as evidence of his arousal. Taking short breaths, she contemplated and wondered. Jon slipped his hand between her legs, cupping her.

"Dessert—hot, sweet, and ready for lapping. Make yourself comfortable, sweets," he whispered hotly against Tina's ear. Jon stroked her swollen clit. Each pulse and throb quivered her fleshy pearl, telegraphing her readiness.

Drake leaned back. Jon knew Drake loved to watch the woman he desired pleasured. Jon agreed there was a certain amount of turn on seeing someone he cared about getting and giving pleasure. Shared voyeurism enhanced things without adding guilt or angst to the play.

Tina glanced from him to Drake. Drake patted the mattress and pillows next to him. "Time to heat things back up."

Jon gave Drake a thumbs-up and cuddled against Tina. "Relax, baby. I'm ready for dessert." Jon licked his lips.

Tina smiled and dropped onto her stomach. Drake reached out as she slightly bounced, patting her ass. He liked Tina's preparation, condoms for several romps and protection for all.

Jon checked the nightstand, noting where he laid the items. He looked up as Drake leaned down to kiss Tina. On his nightstand sat similar items. They were ready. Jon moved to Tina's prior spot. Drake eased her onto her back as they kissed. His hand slowly slid up her leg.

Jon reached for his cock. Cupping his balls with one hand, he encircled his cockhead, squeezed, and stroked down, coating his shaft with pre-cum. He stroked up and down with each movement of Drake's hand higher and closer to Tina's crotch. Jon smiled as he remembered fumbling during their failed threesome with Debbie. Insight and maturity aided for sure.

Drake broke off his and Tina's kiss. He traced the outline of her vulva lips before he plunged his finger between her lips, teasing a light moan out of her. Jon smiled as Drake sniffed and licked his finger. "My friend," Drake began, looking at him. "Your dessert is ready."

Drake helped Tina settle back on the pillows. Her hair lay around her like a crown. Jon sprawled on his stomach between her legs, pulling the lips Drake traced apart, and blew. Tina moaned more, squirming as he blew more. Jon caught her gaze before he dipped his head. Her flushed cheeks and smile delighted him. She indicated her consent. Jon grew harder as he took his first lick.

Chapter Twenty-Six

Drake licked his thumb and forefinger. He captured Tina's nipple between them. Rubbing her tense nipple back and forth, he gently pulled and tugged on his upward caresses.

Jon's head dipped as he slipped between her legs. Lying on his belly, Jon's ass stuck up in the air like a white cloud. Drake smiled as he glanced down Jon's torso to where his feet and lower half of his legs hung off the bed. Not an unusual position if the woman preferred to lie on her back.

Tina's eyes met his and closed as her first moan sounded. Drake's smile deepened with each tremble and sigh she gave. He'd seen Jon bring Debbie to a fevered pitch and frenzy twice during their time with her. Jon studied technique and style, wanting to produce cosmic orgasms to quote him. He would chuckle and add what he liked most about oral sex was the closeness and outcome. Drake understood, inhaling again before he licked his lips. Tina's scrumptious odor filled his nostrils.

Tina jerked as Jon slipped his finger into her. Small continuous ripples of pleasure swarmed over her, leaving her awash in goose bumps and a need for more. "More," she panted, arching her hips and back. "I love..." Her words trailed off.

Bunching the sheet in her hands, she thrust toward Jon. His tongue flicked over, around, and back up to the top of her clit. Drake tugged up on her nipple almost in unison to Jon's laps. In and out, up and down. Every part of her tingled with anticipation of—Tina reached down, threaded her fingers with Jon's hair. She pulled her legs up until her feet were flat on the bed. She lifted her hips, rocking to and fro.

Jon's hands slipped up her ass and hips, cradling her as she rocked tighter to him. Inside her, he rubbed her wet G-spot in what felt like a counter rhythm to his licks. Much more...Tina began humping faster as Jon suckled her clit tightly between his lips. His hold on her hips tightened. He held her in place as he lapped rapidly.

Drake's lips brushed over hers. He let go of her nipple and snuggled closer to her. Drake caught her earlobe between his teeth and nipped.

She arched her neck and she humped Jon's face and tongue as the first wave of climax reached up from the depths. Rolling after rolling wave of orgasm crashed over her. Hotter and more intense than the shower, Tina gave up trying to hold back.

"Oh, my. *Oh my,*" she cried out. "I'm coming."

Jon stilled his strokes on Tina's G-spot. Instead, he applied a light steady pressure. He loosened his suction on her clit, lapping down on her next pulse. Sweetness, sweeter than sugar, tastier than cream, greeted him. He lapped, gathering more of her essence on his tongue and swallowed. Tart and tang met his taste buds. His next taste reminded him of lemon cream pie, sweet with the right amount of tarty tang. Just the way he liked his pie.

He continued cradling her until her frenzied thrusts against him slowed. Jon eased his hands up Tina's back until he supported the small of her back. He pulled away from her, speaking. "I'm here to help you back down to the bed. Let me know when you're ready."

Tina's throaty "okay" added by her stillness gave Jon the indication he needed. "Come down slowly. I've got you," Jon said.

Drake pulled his hand out from beneath Tina as she sank to the bed. Two bouts of hard orgasms for her. Could she withstand another round? He and Jon hadn't come yet.

Tina settled beside him once again on the bed. Her hair lay in clumps and bunches around her. Her flushed cheeks and dewy eyed look grabbed him. Grabbed his crotch and sunk deeper into his heart. He inhaled slowly, watching Jon work his way down the mattress and back up beside Tina on her other side. Drake hadn't planned on getting attached this deeply so soon.

What do you mean soon? his conscience questioned him. Drake pressed his lips together to keep from answering himself out loud. Truth was soon was relative. A year earlier he'd barely met her. Six months ago, Jon and he started getting to know her better. Three months ago, he acknowledged his attraction to her. Jon had, too. The last eight weeks found them together oftener and more frequently. Especially since Nita pulled out of the wedding party. All right, soon no longer fit into the equation. Tina being herself won a good portion of his attention and caring. Tonight his heart spoke about the depth of those feelings.

Drake rolled over to face his nightstand. His balls ached along with his cock. He needed to come. He picked up a condom before rolling back to Tina and Jon. Jon and Tina were wrapped around each other, kissing as if no one else were present.

Tina lay in the crook of Jon's arm, with his hand tangled in her hair. His other hand cupped her breast. Drake could make out one of her arms. They lay so tight to each other there couldn't be any space between them. Jon had one leg over her hip. Tina lay with one of hers over his other leg, their groins skintight together. Drake let go a low whistle. He had his answer about Tina being up to another round. The two rocked back and forth like they were joined balls deep already.

"Um," Drake began, seeing Jon pull back. "Are you two doing what I think you are?"

Jon grinned, shook his head, and eased away from Tina. "No, not yet. Though I think we're ready to."

Drake chuckled, placing his hand in front of him, displaying the condom. "Tonight I want to come deep inside you while you bring Jon off orally."

Drake brought Tina's hand to his lips. He rubbed his cheek over them twice, kissed each, and tipped her palm up. He pressed a kiss there before closing her hand around the kiss. Seeing he had her attention, Drake continued talking.

"Pleasure comes in many forms. I want your pleasure as much as mine. Do you trust me to not hurt you?"

Moments passed without anyone speaking or moving. Tina glanced to Jon, back to Drake. She licked her lips and nodded.

Drake opened her hand and placed the condom there. He lay back with his hands out in front of him. "You're in control. Tell us what you want and how."

Jon rolled over on to his back. "I want to come in your mouth."

Tina wiped her palms on the sheet. Why couldn't some of that moisture be in her mouth and throat instead? Decisions, decisions. Trust mattered with intimacy. Intimacy often resulted due to trust's presence and a high degree of belief and faith in the other person or people. She'd come this far trusting herself, Drake, and Jon as well. Could she go the next step and share in the combined pleasure having the two of them inside her would produce?

She wiped her palms again, blinked, and inhaled slowly. Her heart raced each time she intently looked at the condom. Jon and Drake at the same time? Was fear speaking or anticipation? Maybe both. Information might help ease her angst. She raised her head, her gaze meeting Drake's. She ran her tongue over her lips. Ah, moisture finally. She hoped she didn't sound like a frog.

"Drake, I need..." Tina paused unsure of what to say. There weren't practical words for the info she needed. She sighed and continued. "I don't know which position is best. You know the one that won't hurt."

Drake sat up, crossed his legs, and faced her. "It's different for each person."

Tina worried her lip. Great. How did she find out which one worked for her?

Drake covered her hand with his and spoke. "What didn't work for you?"

Tina nodded. Flashes of her idiot ex grabbing her hips and pushing into her came first followed by a prior guy who got off dominating her with her on her back as he pumped away. No pleasure for her with either. This time she wanted pleasure.

"Little or no pleasure for me." Tina nodded again as she went on. "Very little enjoyment."

Drake shook his head. "I get it. You'll get pleasure. I get off on yours."

Jon slipped his arms around her, hugging her to him. "I remember a position that might work."

Drake arched an eyebrow and shrugged. "Okay. Which one?"

"Doggie style. That gives you leverage from behind." Jon reached down, began stroking her clit, and plucking it with his fingers wet with her cum.

Tina squirmed, rocking her hips. "I'm gonna come," she cried out, pushing back against Jon.

"Beautiful," Drake murmured, capturing her nipple with his lips. He suckled hard while he pinched and rubbed her other nipple.

"Yes, feel it, love. Come for us," Jon whispered excitedly. Tina rocked harder on Jon's fingers, panting as a strong orgasm enveloped her. She cried out, grasping Drake's shoulder, shaking with hard shudders. Her eyes closed. Stars and bright colors burst behind her eyelids. She gulped air while the last wave of gratification claimed her.

"Wow," she managed to get out. She sagged, limp against Jon.

Drake patted her cheek and moved away. "I got the position. Jon on the middle the bed. Tina kneeling facing you. Me from behind."

Jon eased her off him. He made his way around the bed to the foot, sat down, and laid back. He cupped his balls while he stroked his cock. "Come on, darling. I need your wet lips and mouth covering me."

Tina swallowed hard. Drake held his hand out to her. "Our mutual pleasure awaits," he offered.

She moved until she was side-by-side with Jon. Jon winked and puckered. Tina leaned down and brushed her lips over his. Jon jerked, moaning as she fondled him more.

"Need to come. Inside you mouth, please," he moaned. His hands bunched blankets and comforter in them. Tina slid her hand down to his balls, squeezing at the same time. Jon's hips left the bed. His neck arched. His head went back, lifting him off the bed more. She held him steady. Deep into her he went until his balls bumped against her cheeks.

Drake's hot breath flowed down her shoulders and back.

"Easy. On your next move lean forward more." Drake eased one finger into her.

Jon spread his legs wider, giving Drake room to get closer. Jon began thrusting in and out of her mouth.

Drake touched her. "Hold steady. I'm partway in."

Tina clenched vagina. Fear threatened to spill out. How had Drake managed this?

"It's okay," Drake soothed, running his hands up and down her back. "You relaxed into this. You can again."

Tina shivered. Jon copied his caresses on each of her nipples with one hand while cupping her head with his other. Drake leaned into her more. Thickness filled her, causing brief fissures of pain, igniting bursts of pleasure. Slowly she rocked back, reminding herself to relax.

"A bit more," Drake groaned. "Oh, god, you're tight. So tight."

Drake's balls and legs slapped against her. He pumped into her, gradually easing partway out. He countered Jon's thrusting.

Deep within her, the quake began. Shudders, tremors, and intense feelings poured over her. Her nipples tightened. Her clit constricted. Rapture grasped her, tossed her upward, only to land in the largest tsunami orgasmic wave of the night.

Drake and Jon pumped in and out of her simultaneously. So full. Tighter than ever before. Chockfull of two cocks. Wonderfully hot hard maleness plummeting into her until...

Jon let go of nipple. He reached up and held her head and thrust twice into her mouth. "Gonna come. *Now*," he cried out.

Behind her, Drake gripped her firmer. "Oh yes. *Me, too*," he shouted.

Dual semen spurted deep into her. Tina tightened once more and cried out, rocking back and forth until she collapsed on Jon.

Chapter Twenty-Seven

Tina spooned to Jon, drawing the covers over them. She yawned again. Neither of them had to be to work until ten today. The last week had flown by. Drake was due back today from his ten-day business trip.

"Hey." She giggled. "That tickles."

"I'd rather tickle this," Jon quipped. He reached between her legs, fondling her pubis. He probed lower, finding her clit.

He nipped her neck with his stroke. Tina arched against Jon. "It's six-thirty. Do we have time?"

"Yes," he whispered, nipping her again. "Yes, we do."

Tina felt Jon roll away from her. She pulled the sheet up over her bare arms and shoulders. She smiled, remembering she slept nude. Two weeks ago, she wore pajamas or a night shirt to bed. A lot had happened in the last fourteen days.

Their first night together flowed into two days spent discussing them. Them as a trio. Them as two separate couples. Them as individuals. The outcome was clear. More talks and disclosures would come. For now, they agreed three together time happened as schedules and need allowed. Over nights became evident within the first week. Drake's office closed at 6:00 p.m. where Jon stayed open late Tuesday and Thursday to accommodate his clients. Tina knew her time with Frank was ending soon. Her last classes began in September, eight weeks from now. Changes flowed and nudged them into a loosely knit rhythm of two to three nights together here and there.

Tina felt the bed dip as Jon climbed back in beside her. He pressed against her. "Lift your leg, sweetums. Let me slide into your warm wetness."

Tina lifted her leg and pressed back against Jon. Her dampness oozed out, lubricating her more. Essence of last night's lovemaking filled the air. Jon's chest filled as he inhaled. "Love that scent," he teased, entering her more.

Tina's giggles turned to moans and sighs. The bed moved in time with their short jousts and thrusts. Sounds of a hand swatting flesh began. Tina moaned more with each swat Jon delivered. Jon picked up the pace. Each swat tightened her around him. He whispered of his next move as he surged into her. "On your hands and knees."

Jon pulled out, rolling away from her. Tina scrambled to her hands and knees. She looked to where Jon stood. Shivers rushed over her. Memories of her second night with Drake and Jon flushed her. Each taught her new meanings of pleasure. Jon taught her prolonged foreplay ramped-up the results higher. Last night their lovemaking took a new turn.

"And now our toys, my pretty," Jon said. Tina groaned as he laid the concentrator on the bed. Nipple clamps joined by a chain lead to another longer chain with a single similar clamp. She jerked as a low whirling sound began. Jon held out a finger covered with a fingertip vibrator.

Jon walked to the foot of the bed, laying back so he was under her. He stroked her clit, tweaking her with his thumb and forefinger. Her wetness grew with each touch. Jon pulled her vulva lips apart and blew. Tina rocked toward him. He held her hips, lapping and sampling her dewiness. A small orgasm rippled through her. He stopped. Still rubbing her clit, he moved upward. Suckling her nipples until they resembled her swollen clit, he clamped them close to her areolas. He tugged the chain as he slid back the bed until he reached her pubis again. Two quick strokes on her clit left her panting and trembling. He smiled, winked, and clamped her clit.

Tina groaned deeper with each stroke of the fingertip vibrator over, around, and close to her clit and nipples. Jon worked her close to one orgasm, then another. Each time he backed off. How much more could she withstand?

The bed dipped behind her. One swat then another sounded, warming her ass cheeks. Jon leaned against her. He was harder than when they first started. He pushed deep, holding her firm. Tina pushed back, breathing, and relaxing.

"Gosh, you are so tight. I love this," Jon moaned, sliding balls deep into her. He loosened his hold on her, leaned over her, and began stroking her clit in time to his thrusts.

Her bed squeaked and rocked with them echoing their moans and throaty groans. Jon picked up the pace as she tightened around him, rocking back and forth. His balls slapped against her, edging her closer to the hard mind-blowing orgasms she'd learned to enjoy. Jon tugged on the concentrator midway down, it sending spirals of light pain coursing over her.

Who knew the man knew how close pain and pleasure ran. Drake smiled when Jon asked permission to teach Tina about the edginess of lovemaking. His permission and admonishment to take good care of her before he left on his business trip caught Tina off guard. Since then, under Jon's loving tutelage, she knew kink had its place in their sexuality. Drake liked a bit of restraint in theirs. Restraining him added to her own pleasure in ways Tina hadn't known about until she tried. Yes, both men had their individual styles and preferences. Together as three, their play and loving took on gentler easier nature. Tina enjoyed each aspect.

Tina rocked back against Jon. "I'm coming," she purred, dipping her head. She shook harder, shuddering with each pounding pulse of the orgasm rocketing up her groin, pulsing her clit and nipples. Jon's groaned "uh-huh" sounded behind her. He held her firm again, pumping rapidly in and out of her. Tina grabbed bunches of the sheet in her hands. Huge waves of scalding delight engulfed her. Jon thrust into her, held still, and groaned, "Me, too."

Both fell to the bed, joined and sated. Moments passed until their breathing returned to near normal. Jon quickly removed the clamps. He suckled each nipple causing more jerks and moans. He feathered light caresses around her clit until her post orgasmic movements subsided. Tina glanced at the clock as Jon pulled the sheet over them. They had forty minutes to nap.

Drake glanced at his watch. Ten minutes until he boarded his flight home. Ten days away and he wanted to celebrate after he slept in his own bed. In his own bed with Tina nude, snuggled to him. Jealousy didn't begin to describe the feelings running through him. He wanted time alone with Tina, time to reconnect and recharge their connection. Envy came to mind each time he examined his feelings and reactions. When he talked to Jon and Tina the last time, his stomach refused to settle. Nor would his heart stop racing each time she giggled and chided Jon for tickling her. Yes, he was envious. An emotion that did him good in acknowledging his feelings. He trusted Jon. Drake knew his trust level with Tina grew and increased each time they talked.

The last text from his cell phone company showed him over the limits of his plan. Drake smiled, knowing that in two hours home was a thirty minute drive away. Adding Tina to his cell phone plan worked. Even Jon agreed. Her phone died the first night she returned home from their three days together. Anxious to make sure she was fine, both he and Jon showed up at her place individually with the same thought in mind. Check on her and notify the other. That night lead to another together crowded in her bed. As much as he craved time alone with Tina, he missed Jon, too.

The loud speaker crackled, followed by the announcement to begin boarding. Drake picked up his briefcase, computer bag, and jacket. His cell phone rang as he started down the causeway. By the time he got settled in his seat, he barely had time to check who the call was from. The message to buckle up and turn off electronic devices came all too quickly.

Tina snagged her cell phone out of her purse. Pushing her cart down the crowded grocery store aisle, she shouldered the phone against her ear. "Hey Janet! I didn't expect you back until tomorrow."

Janet's soft sigh echoed through the ear piece. "We're not. I needed to talk to you before we got back in port."

Tina shoved her cart off to the side near the pharmacy section of the store, taking a seat in one of their waiting area chairs. "I'm all ears."

Janet's muffled voice filtered through before she spoke clearly. Tina made out bits and pieces of manners and family obligations. Good gods in heaven, the dragoness and her motley crew had escaped their lair.

"Mrs. Daniels," Janet began. "Spent the better part of the last week driving my parents and relatives bat shit crazy."

Tina covered her mouth, hoping to stifle her mirth. Poor Janet. How badly had the dragoness and her cohorts singed Janet's parents and relatives? Two weeks without more than a passing voice mail from the battleax was sheer nirvana. Now Tina knew who kept busy dousing the flamethrower.

"Oh, my. How can I help?" Tina offered, knowing damage control didn't top the list. Damage was already done from the tone of Janet's next words.

"Help we'll discuss in a few days. Locate Drake and Jon for me. Rodger wants to talk to them later on." Janet continued briefly before closing.

Tina ended the call shaking her head. Thanks to static in the connection along with a loud roar plus a bad echo, she caught a few words. Family meeting and wedding on. Shit, engaging in battle again with the dragoness and her horde wasn't going to be easy.

Slipping her phone into her purse, Tina noticed the time. She had a couple of hours until Drake's flight landed. His tone during his last call worried her. He mentioned more than once alone time and her. While he discussed missing Jon, too, Tina wondered if the green-eyed jealousy monster spoiled a fight, also.

"Dragons, green-eyed monsters, and two boyfriends, oh my," she quipped, glancing at her shopping list. Partway down the aisle, she looked back over her shoulder. Two elderly women stood gawking at her with their mouths open. Tina waved and continued on with her marketing.

Drake unfastened his seatbelt. Turbulence, rowdy kids, and Mrs. McNichols with oodles of pictures of her grandchildren aside, he didn't mind waiting to exit the plane. He pulled his jacket on and took his computer and briefcase out of the overhead bin. On the opposite side of the airport, the woman he loved waited for him. If his luggage made the claim area before he did, great. Maybe he could avoid Mrs. McNichols and more of her fervent matchmaking attempts.

Tina circled the arrival area, watching for Drake. His text said door seven. She slowed, making her way toward the inner lane passing closest to the terminal area. She could make him out as he exited the terminal. His smile grew and his wave became more animated. There was no doubt Drake was glad to be home.

"Hi, love," he called out, opening the back passenger side door. "Thanks for picking me up." He tossed his suitcase and carryon items on the seat. Quickly closing the door, he nearly vaulted into the front seat next to her. He faced her, buckling his seatbelt. "It's great to see you. Now please get me out of here."

Drake kept looking back as she made her way into traffic and away from the crowded arrival area. Ten minutes passed before he slumped in the seat letting out a loud sigh. "Thanks for saving me."

Tina chortled at Drake's wink and lusty grin. "Do I dare ask what I saved you from?"

"A matchmaking grandmother who doesn't get subtlety."

"Speaking of subtly, guess who I heard from?" Tina glimpsed at Drake before she continued.

He shrugged, laying his hand on her outer thigh. "Jon left a voice mail saying Rodger and Janet needed to meet with us."

"Janet called me today. Bad connection didn't help. Best I could make out was family meeting and wedding on."

Drake cussed and sat up. "Fuck, Aunt Helen strikes again."

"Yes, the dragoness and her minion escaped their lair," Tina added, entering the highway.

"No doubt there's crap to handle," Drake offered, patting her leg.

"Janet's bad connection didn't help. She did say her family and relatives felt the flames, too." Tina pulled into the high-speed lane, turned on cruise control, and looked at Drake.

His hair stood up in places from him rubbing his head on the seat as he shook his head no. She grinned. Memories of their last night together filtered to the top of her thoughts. Yes, seeing his hair like that due to him thrashing and groaning with pleasure was definitely more enjoyable. From the side, she could make out the faint dark circles under his eyes along with the shadow of his beard stubble. Poor man needed a good night's sleep after a rousing session of lovemaking. Was he up for what she had in mind? Crock pot lasagna, garlic bread, and Caesar salad first. A glass or two of wine with dinner followed by her surprise came second. A few new play toys might get broken in if Drake got the second wind she hoped for.

"Aunt Helen's become a loose cannon," Drake began. "Rodger texted me last week his dad filed for divorce."

Tina turned off the highway onto Lakeshore Drive. "Wow, I heard the chatter the night of the party. I figured the results were none of my business."

Drake chuckled. "You and everyone else within hearing distance. I guess we'll know soon enough what's going down."

Tina nodded, parking the car. "For sure. Tonight's for us. Jon is over at his sister's, babysitting."

Drake laughed harder as he got his stuff out of the car. "Glad it's him and not me. He adores his nieces and nephew. They're a handful."

Chapter Twenty-Eight

Drake carefully sat his half-full wine glass on the table next to his recliner. He dropped into the chair, sinking down into the plush leather almost sighing. Cushioned, replete with a full stomach, and slow jazz wafting through the room from the CD player, he relaxed, willing all his muscles from his stiff shoulders down to the bottom of his feet and toes to let go. No more being on, having to make decisions, discuss strategies, look at calendars, or even take charge beyond the confines of his home. Tomorrow would bring that soon enough. Monday morning and his first day...he glanced to where Tina sat on the couch with her legs tucked beneath her. She watched him as she sipped her wine.

Drake picked up his glass of wine, swirled the contents, and held the glass aloft, speaking. "Here's to being a business owner."

Tina spit, sputtered, covered her mouth with her hand. She placed her glass on the table behind the couch. Her eyes widened as his words sunk in. She looked away. Back at him and stood. Her fisted hands landed on her hips. There was no mistaking the glare and fire in her eyes as she approached.

"What do you mean business owner?" Tina stopped when she reached the edge of the coffee table. She reached toward the couch. Drake quickly sat his glass on the table, hoping it was well out of the way.

One, then another pillow volleyed at him. He caught the smaller ones tossing them back at Tina. Two plopped on the floor next to her. She drew back with a larger one in her hand. "Well, are you going to answer me?"

Drake sat upright, pressing his lips tightly together. If he laughed, Tina might toss the firmer throw pillows at him. Those could knock things off tables and leave more mess than he cared to deal with tonight.

"Easy, darlin'," he began, moving to the edge of his chair. "I'll explain, but first you put the ammo down. Okay?"

Drake held his hands up in front of him, palms out. He took several deep breaths waiting for Tina's next move. He knew he caught her by surprise. He hadn't anticipated her outburst. He placed his palms on his legs. He counted and watched. Five-four-three...Crap! He rocked back, shaking his head. Right before he left, he and Jon kidded about becoming partners if he expanded his business. The last discussion included Tina joining them in the venture.

Drake rose. Keeping Tina in his view, he moved toward her. "It's not what you think. Jon and I aren't business partners."

Tina blew her hair off her face. Her frown and furled brow said her ire hadn't cooled. Drake licked his lips and stepped closer to her. He continued talking. "Remember I mentioned my meeting with the regional VP?"

"Yes." Tina perched on the arm of the couch. Her glare softened some. Drake kept talking.

"He offered me directorship of the Cascade Bay office. Since I've headed up the larger projects and built business up, he wants me in charge." Drake walked forward until he stood tight to Tina. He leaned down, brushed his lips over hers, and smiled.

Tina looked up at him. Her features relaxed. She chewed her lip as if in thought. She reached up, tucking her hair behind one ear. She nodded, then spoke. "Congrats, dear. How soon do you know?"

Drake chuckled. "It's already official, love." He cupped Tina's chin. Staring into her eyes he finished. "Signed the papers this morning before I flew out."

She cuffed him on his arm, softly chastising him. "Drake, you rascal. I'm happy for you. Congrats, baby."

Tina scooted to the edge of the arm, slipping her arms around his waist hugging him to her. Drake sighed as he rested his chin on top of her head, hugging her back. He sagged against her, glad to be home and in the arms of the woman he cherished. Knowing she cherished him too added to the warmth and depth of emotions rolling through him.

"How about we celebrate by going to bed..." Tina let her voice trail off. She tilted her head back, looking to see if she had Drake's attention. His gaze met hers. A small grin grew at her next words. "And have some fun with a surprise I have for you."

She watched Drake's throat work as he swallowed. His Adam's apple bobbed twice for each swallow he took. She had his attention. Placing her hands on his chest, she pushed on him. "Well, yes or no?"

Drake's grin grew into a smile with him vigorously nodding yes. Tina knew where she wanted the evening to end up. Taking charge turned her on as much as submitting did. How she turned out being a switch she didn't know. Thank goodness for the internet and search engines. She understood this developing different side of herself better as a result.

Tina rose, slipping her hand into Drake's. There was something so right about the warmth of the person she cared about in the palm of her hand. Touching her deep inside. Deep within her heart and core. This morning the same thing happened as Jon embraced her before he left. Soft "I care" turned into "I love you" somewhere within the last weeks. Overanalyzing wasn't going to change a thing. Love happened of its own accord. Not because someone or something predicted it. Sometimes a person had to go with the flow and trust their heart and gut to lead them the right way. Tina knew hers was leading her forward into new and unique territory. She understood change. This change she embraced and valued. She got Jon and Drake as a result.

"Come on, my submissive one. Tonight I'm in charge of our mutual pleasure." Tina started down the hall leading to her bedroom with Drake trailing behind her. Yes, tonight his pleasure was hers to command and direct.

She grinned as they entered the bedroom. On top of the bed, across her pillows, two silk scarves lay knotted together. Would Drake submit? Give her permission to take the lead in their mating?

Tina glanced over her shoulder. Drake stood close to her. He appeared to be scanning the bed. She swallowed hard, waiting for some sign of his reaction. From the side, an unclear view permitted no clarity of understanding. She moved back until she stood beside Drake and spoke. "If you prefer, we can forego this?"

Drake stepped to the bed and leaned down.

Gasping scarves, he pulled them to him. He turned facing her. He knelt on both knees and looked up. His gaze met hers. He raised his hands, palms up, offering her the scarves.

"Your wish, Mistress?" he voiced, his tone low and subdued.

Tina leaned down, brushing her lips over Drake's. She took the scarves from him. "Hands out in front of you. Wrists together."

Drake complied, presenting his hands and wrists close together. "Not too tight, please, Mistress."

Tina nodded, loosely looping the scarves around Drake's hands and forearms. She tied the ends in a loose square knot. "Pain is so close to pleasure. One that can go either way."

Drake nodded. "I prefer pleasure."

Tina smiled. "Me, too, dear. Nothing too edgy I hope."

Drake rose, moving back until he reached the bed. He dropped onto the mattress, bouncing slightly as he sat. Tina followed him. Drake reached out to catch her.

"Keep your hands where I can see them," she scolded. Drake shook his head and looked down. Tina didn't miss the smile and wink before he looked away.

"Yes, too eager." The next move was up to her.

She moved in front of Drake, grasped his chin, and tilted his head back until she could see his eyes. Yes, time to take charge.

"Stand up," she said, taking ahold of Drake's bound hands, pulling him to her. She reached for his belt, unfastening it as she spoke. "Too dressed for my likes. Way too dressed."

Tina shoved Drake's pants down around his knees. Next came first one button, then another, followed by others. Soon his dress shirt hung open, framing his undershirt, showing his washboard abs and toned pecs. Her gaze swept lower. The elastic of his silk briefs came into view. A smile formed as she remembered his initial reaction when she presented each of them a pair after their first weekend together. Jon hemmed and hawed about putting his on. Drake had stripped and modeled his for her. He even wiggled his ass and twerked amidst Jon's catcalls and whistles.

Running her hand up and over, she traced the exposed area his open shirt provided. With each pass she came closer to her prizes, his swollen cock and balls. Tina licked two fingers before she rubbed her hand firmly upward across Drake's chest until she reached the buds of his nipples. Capturing them between her slick fingers, she pulled and tweaked, copying his previous moves to hers. She leaned into him, pressing her lips on the warm male flesh her questing hands exposed with each upward bunch of his shirt. Bit by bit, stroke by stroke, bare male skin came into view. There was no mistaking Drake's state of desire.

"Getting to you, am I?" Tina teased, nipping her way up Drake's chest toward his neck. She skimmed her hand downward, stopping at the waistband of his briefs. She eased her fingers under the band, stroking downward until soft hair caressed her fingertips.

Drake jerked as she reached lower. Tina ran her palm over the tip of his cock, wetting her fingers and palm with his juices. She pulled her hand away, licking her palm and fingers. She let go with her other hand, dropping the shirt bunches she held. Placing both hands, palms down, on Drake's chest, she pushed him backward.

Drake dropped back onto the bed. He sat, looked up, and smiled. Tina stood a few feet from him. Her hands went to the buttons at the waist of her capris. One then another came undone, followed by the zipper until they sagged on her hips, showing mauve and teal colored lace. More color and sateen material came into view as Tina shoved her capris down her hips, over her thighs until the pants pooled around her ankles. Drake swallowed hard as his heart beat faster. Tina turned around and bent over giving him full view of the thong panties he'd sent her from San Francisco. The view as she bent over more set off sparks, lighting a roman candle that he hoped she soon doused. Some of the heat his cock and balls kept sputtering and spitting, leaked deep into his groin, threatening to erupt into a huge need to claim her. Take her without much more foreplay. Not a satisfying turn of events. Mutual pleasure shared by two multiplied the satisfaction factor significantly.

"Babe," he began, raising his bound wrists as Tina kicked her capris away. "Can't undress me further with these on me."

Tina nodded, pulling her top over her head and dropped it on top of her capris. The plunge bra she wore matched her panties. Drake inhaled sharply. He'd brought the bra, sight unseen, based on a suggestion from the clerk when he ordered the panties from the specialty lingerie shop he found near Fisherman's Wharf. The plunge drew his eyes where he expected it would. Her cleavage tantalized him in ways he hadn't thought about until now. Some oil and a bit of rubbing...God, coming that way would be exciting. Maybe she could suckle him between her lips when he stroked toward her.

"Yes, there are limits aren't there," Tina quipped, moving away from him. She stopped near her nightstand, bent over, and shook her ass from side to side. Drake tried to breathe and swallow. His throat constricted as Tina straightened and opened the nightstand drawer. The minx had his attention. If his cock got any harder, he'd come from the sheer thought of sinking balls deep into her. What games did she have in mind? Any edgier and he would be aching and needing multiple releases.

Drake waited, taking shallow breaths. He watched Tina's hand dip into the drawer. Her movements indicated she looked for something. Moments passed, tightening his balls tighter to him. His horny id began tossing fantasy pictures into his thoughts. Coherent actions and replies weren't going to function much longer.

Tina spun around, holding her hands out in front of her. "You choose how many. I decide what position."

She must have three to four condoms in the palm of her hands. Drake tried to not snort as he exhaled. He'd be lucky to last long enough to use one. More than that...not tonight. Now in the morning, that was another time and place.

"One, darlin', is all I can handle tonight. Choose your fave position and let's start pleasuring." Drake held up his bound hands again. "Please?"

Tina stood with her arms crossed, her eyes rolled upward as though she were in deep thought. Drake closed his eyes, shaking his head. He noticed the impish grin curving her lips from the moment he told her choose her fave position. She had two, woman on top and on her hands and knees with him under her eating her out which often lead to them sixty-nining.

"Ok, once is good. And—" Tina looked down. Drake sent a short prayer heavenward his adorable minx would let him off the ledge soon. He wanted to come inside her, not all over himself and his briefs.

Tina tossed the other condoms back in the drawer. She turned back to Drake. "As soon as I'm undressed, we get you naked."

Tina reached behind her, slowly unfastening her bra. She slumped one shoulder then her other. Drake groaned, wanting to tug the offensive article of clothing off her and out of her reach. He licked his lips, ready to speak their agreed safe word when she tossed the bra at him. He ducked and rose to find her beautifully nude before him. She cupped her breasts, thumbing her nipples as she walked to him. "Now you can sample these," she offered, leaning forward, holding her breasts close to his mouth.

Drake caught her as she leaned over more. He cupped his hands, supporting her as best he could. He suckled the nipple closest to him, eliciting a moan and murmurs of pleasure growing in intensity the harder he sucked. He glanced upward, watching as Tina dropped her head back and her eyes closed. Her grip on his shoulder tightened. She began to quiver. Her orgasm wasn't far off. Drake let go of her nipple. Tonguing the sensitive tip, he leaned back, checking the location of her other breast. Sighting the cousin of the fleshy nub he blew on, he scooted sideways a bit and repeated his loving administrations to the other. He could feel Tina's every vocal appreciation and response as her body and flesh reacted. A few more suckles and licks, she would come. Watching her pleasure swarm over her and take her higher until she pinnacled into a crescendo of smaller orgasms turned him on. Pleasuring her to several pinnacles with Jon's assistance amplified the return for everyone. Tonight was for Tina and him. A night Drake planned to end with both of them sated and fulfilled. He knew he couldn't take much more before he started to lose his edge on his desire.

Drake loosened his hold on Tina's other nipple. He kissed each breast before speaking. "Love, please untie me. I'm aching to sink deep into you and soak within your warmth."

Tina blinked, shook her head, and gazed at him. She seemed to be lost in a post-orgasmic haze. He'd gotten to her. Good. Now maybe he wouldn't need to use their safe word. Not that their play got that heavy into the BDSM-sphere. Tina nodded and stepped back. She reached down quickly untying his wrists. She tossed the scarves over her shoulder. She kept humming some jaunty tune. He couldn't quite make it out.

Drake stood, rubbed his wrists, and stripped. His clothes landed next to Tina's on the floor. As he bent down to finish easing his briefs and socks off, Tina's humming grew in volume. She muttered a few of the words as he straightened up.

"All around the bench." Tina grinned and lunged at him.

Drake fell back on the bed, bouncing some as he hit the mattress. Tina stood between his legs, grinning merrily at him. He shrugged and worked his way back further on the bed. Encircling his cock with his hand, he stroked down to his balls and back. Cum oozed out of him, coating his cockhead and fingers. "Don't waste a good thing, darlin'," he offered, spreading his legs wider. Tina grabbed the condom package, tore it open, and kneeled on the bed.

Drake groaned as she squeezed him, working the condom down and over him. Tina straddled him. Inch by inch she engulfed him with her warm wetness. Drake gripped the bedspread as he clenched his hands, bunching mounds of it against his palms. One flex, then another followed by more until he lost count. How many times didn't matter. Tina milked him with her Kegel movements. The warmth and contractions ramped him higher and hotter toward his own pinnacle of climax. Then she stopped.

Lord, what was his impish minx doing to him? Take him along the ledge to the edge and leave him hanging? Tantalizing him until he couldn't hold back and cried out with his own release?

Tina leaned forward, resting her hands on Drake's stomach. Her own release pounded in her ears, demanding the orgasm she wanted and knew Drake sought for her. She wanted the same for him. A tremendous blowout that left them with little energy and mental clarity other than to drop into the bed spooned together as sleep claimed them.

She rose and tightened around him. Rocking slightly back, she slipped down him until his balls bumped her. Tightening more, she rocked and rode, repeating her movements until their mutual vocals of pleasure mixed together. On her next upward move, she asked for his assistance. "Play with my clit. I want a double orgasm."

Drake reached between her pussy lips, coating his fingers with her juices. One, then two fingers accompanied by others circled around and over her taut, pulsating clit. Tina picked up the pace of her ride. Drake's eyes closed. His neck arched. A deep groan rolled out of him as he lifted his hips off the bed, meeting her on her downward stroke. Tina gasped. White light clouded her vision. Wave after huge wave of thunderous ecstasy swamped her, taking her deep within its whirlpool. Unable to contain her enthusiasm, she cried out as two more waves crashed over her. Limpness claimed her. The whirlpool of her orgasm ebbed and drained away. She fell forward, caught by Drake as she crashed. He cradled her against him, brushing her hair off her face.

Moments passed until their breathing returned to normal allowing them to summon small amounts of energy and strength to untangle themselves from each other. Drake peeled off the condom dropping it in the bathroom wastebasket before urinating. He yawned as Tina quickly washed her hands and face after using the toilet. Leaning against each other, they made their way into the bedroom. Soon their soft breathing filled the quiet darkness surrounding them. Replete and sated sleep claimed them.

Chapter Twenty-Nine

Tina looked around the dining room table. Where had the last week gone? Between Drake assuming ownership of his office, now a franchise owner thanks to his employer, and Jon's pickup in business, the last seven days flew by. Hyacinth needed an extra month off. Her leave offered Tina more than enough hours to officially quit Frank.

Rodger and Janet sat closest to the kitchen. Janet stood and walked into the kitchen. "Continue talking. I'm checking on the roast."

Drake picked up his beer glass, drank, and nodded. He sat opposite Tina. She smiled as Jon squeezed her hand under the table. They sat side-by-side, arriving before Drake had.

Rodger sighed and drummed his fingers on the table. "My mother can be a royal pain in the ass!" he lamented, tossing his drink coaster on the table like a Frisbee.

"I agree," Janet called out from the kitchen. "A week and half at sea with no cell phone or internet available, sheer nirvana. Then we got in range…" Her voice trailed off.

Rodger nodded. "The phone began chiming and ringing almost nonstop it seemed."

Janet rejoined them, sitting down. "We had to turn the phones off. Otherwise our last few idyllic days would have jumped overboard from that woman and her sic'ing everyone she could on us."

"Well," Tina began. "What can we do to help?"

Janet smiled, shook her head, and laughed. "Tell me you haven't altered your maid of honor dress."

Tina squinted, frowned, and gave Janet a raspberry. "Pfffft. Why do you ask?"

Rodger chortled. "Parents. You got 'em. You need 'em. And they can be problematic, in-laws or your own."

Janet grabbed Rodger's ear. "Mind your manners. I get to bitch about mine first. Then you can."

Rodger nodded. Tina caught Drake's smirk and Jon's bemused smile out of the corner of her eye. The dragoness and her motely minions hadn't achieved much except to strengthen the bond between Janet and Rodger.

Janet sipped her wine and continued from where she left off. "Sometimes my parents can be big sticklers on propriety and manners like Rodger's are. So—"

Janet looked around the table and elbowed Rodger who sat staring off into space. He jumped and finished her statement. "The blasted church shindigs are on."

Drake rocked back in his chair, sputtering his mouthful of beer down his chin. He grabbed the napkin next to him, wiped his mouth, and clapped his hands, palms down, on the table. "What the hell prompted this?"

"I'd like to know, too," Jon added.

Janet rose, motioning them toward the kitchen. "Food's done. Let's fill our plates and we'll talk more while we eat."

Fifteen minutes later, they sat around the table again, eating and resuming their discussion.

Janet cleared her throat. Tina set her knife and fork down. She didn't need to choke on a mouthful of food if more surprises were coming. Tina picked up her water glass and hastily drank. She swallowed quickly as Janet started talking.

"Like I said before my parents, like Rodger's, are sticklers for decorum. And this time, they're dogging us like Rodger's mother is." Janet forked food into her mouth and started chewing.

Rodger spoke next. "We figure to keep the peace so we're going to go through the charade of the church floor show and pageantry. Since we paid for the reception, no one gets to change that."

Drake nodded. He spoke in between bites of food. "Makes sense. Aunt Helen doesn't take no for an answer. God, what a prig she can be."

Jon chuckled. "You put it nicely Drake. A real killjoy. Rodger, I'm in. Standing up with you at the church is a small price to keep Aunt Helen from driving you more ape shit."

Rodger looked at Janet. Tina kept eating, knowing that look from the things Janet confided to her when she and Rodger started dating. Janet's stern look and steely-eyed gaze foretold there was an undercurrent happening. Rodger shook his head "no" a couple of times. Janet nodded and mouthed "yes" twice.

"Either you tell them or I will," Janet said. Her tone and harsh pitch had everyone's attention. Tina watched Drake and Jon put their utensils down. Both wiped their mouths, turning in their chairs to be able to see Rodger better.

"Well, you gonna tell them or am I?" Janet asked, laying her fork on her plate. "Rodger, they've got a right to know."

Rodger sighed, and nodded. He stood and tossed his napkin on the table. He paced to the end of the dining room and back to his chair. His shoulders slumped as he dropped back into his chair.

"Yes, they need to know."

Tina reached for Jon's hand. He entwined his fingers with hers. Whatever Rodger needed to share, from his apparent angst and posture, it wasn't good. Tina glanced to Drake. He winked and nodded. He understood her quiet concern. *Poor Rodger* kept running through her mind. His pompous dragon mother and challenging family members aside, Tina truly liked him.

Rodger straightened up, cleared his throat, and spoke. "Kristen and her wife eloped on mother as well. They made the San Francisco Chronicle's society page, complete with pictures and nuptial details."

Tina shook her head as she squeezed Jon's hand. Drake sent her an airborne kiss while Janet comforted Rodger.

"Tell them the rest, hon. Between us, we'll get things figured out." Janet leaned over, hugged Rodger again, and went back to eating.

"Mother and Dad are...shit, filed...ah, fuck it. They're divorcing." Rodger gulped the remaining third of his wine. He gently set the glass on the table. Rocking forward, he placed his hands on the table and sighed. "They're living in separate wings of the house."

Drake smirked, chortled, and snorted. "Talk about a whirlwind of shit happening."

"Amen on that one, brother," Jon added.

"So back to what are *we* going to do?" Tina voiced. Janet nodded empathically.

"Before we go there, I think Janet and Rodger need to know about us." Drake stood, picking up his plate and utensils. "I suggest we have coffee or tea and cake in the living room where we'll be more comfortable."

Drake and Jon accompanied Rodger into the living room to make room for talking and dessert. Janet cornered Tina in the kitchen as she helped put away the leftovers. "Tina, what's Drake talking about?"

Tina shrugged. "I'm not sure. He's got something he wants you to know. Remember I gave up reading minds."

Janet scowled as she put the last container of leftovers in the refrigerator. "I don't need any more dark surprises, okay?"

Tina chuckled. "I doubt it's anything like that. Quite a bit happened while you were gone. Let's go see what he has to say."

Janet turned on the dishwasher. Tina carried the tray with coffee cups and cake plates on it into the living room. Janet followed with the cake and coffee server. Janet leaned down and whispered something to Rodger. He got up and followed her into the kitchen.

Drake took the tray from Tina, setting it on the coffee table midway between the couch and the three chairs surrounding it. As she turned, Jon patted the cushion next to him on the couch. "Come sit between us."

Tina gawped at him, wide-eyed. This was the first they were outing themselves. Letting others know about their trio. Triad was the word Drake used in their latest conversations on how to describe their relationship configuration. She knew Janet and Rodger deserved to know. A bit more advanced warning beyond Drake's statement moments ago might have eased her butterfly-filled stomach. Tina took a deep breath and answered. "All right."

Drake sat next to her, loosely laying his arm across her shoulders. Jon laid his hand on her upper thigh, close to where her shorts stopped. There was no mistaking their ease with each other and the guys' displays of affection and intent.

Janet sat the serving plate holding cake slices on the table. Rodger held a smaller tray holding a cream pitcher and sugar bowl along with spoons and forks. No one spoke while Janet served cake and coffee. As she sat, she spoke. "Drake, Rodger and I got your silent message. You and Jon are..."

"Seeing Tina," Drake finished for Janet. He sipped his coffee in between bites of cake.

Rodger kept forking cake into his mouth. He nodded and chewed. Janet pointed her fork at Jon. "And you are?"

"Great with it. I've got no problems with them being together." Jon jerked his thumb toward Tina and Drake.

"Tina?" Janet asked, leaning forward.

"I'm fine. Really okay with both of them." Tina finished her cake, put her plate on the empty tray, and started drinking her coffee.

Rodger added his empty mug and plate to the growing pile on the tray. He slipped his around Janet's waist, hugging her to him. "Sweetie, remember we discussed setting Tina up with Drake or Jon for the party."

"Yeah. What about it?"

"One of our what ifs was the three of them together." Rodger perched on the arm of the couch. "I wasn't sure after Debbie if Jon and Drake would give sharing another try."

Drake chortled. "Rodger, Jon and I never gave up hope. We decided to try different approaches."

"Those didn't pan out either for a joint venture." Jon stretched as he spoke. "We're happy with Tina."

Tina stood as Janet came around the couch. "I'm happy with them. I'll help you clear this up."

Ten minutes later, they settled back to resume their dinner discussion. Rodger spoke first. "We're okay with you three as a unit. The rest of the wedding party and family may not be."

Janet nodded, holding up her hand when Drake opened his mouth to speak. "There's no need to tell anyone. If they ask, tell 'em the truth. You're there together. More than that is none of their business."

Tina, Jon, and Drake agreed.

"Now to answer your earlier question, Drake. Why this happened." Janet slumped down into the overstuffed chair she sat in, kicking off her shoes and perching her feet up on the table. "My parents along with Rodger's feel this way—" Janet paused, nudging Rodger.

Rodger jumped. "Sorry, I'm still trying to understand why my parents took until now to file for divorce."

Janet patted her husband's arm. "Dear, just like my parents are dogging us about propriety and following through."

Tina leaned forward, holding out her hand. "I can sum things up in two words, money and manners."

Janet smiled and pointed at her. "Bingo! We got a winner. Both parents and RSVPs for guests attending the function."

Jon snorted as he stood, yawning and stretching. "So we got folks attending, family pushing and prodding for this to go forth. Seems to me least we can do Drake is stand up for Rodger and help him out."

Jon continued speaking as he sat back down. "Logistics, please."

Janet sat up and fished in her shorts pocket. She pulled out a folded piece of paper. She smoothed out the folds and ran her finger down the writing on the page. "Nathan is still in. With you and Drake, Tina and—oh, Wynona is the only bridesmaid who didn't quit on me. That gives us seven, including us."

"Who's escorting who?" Jon held out his hand for the paper Janet passed to Tina.

"I'm going down the aisle myself. My family and Rodger's will be seated before the procession starts." Janet snuggled up to Rodger, who sat on the arm of the chair next to her.

"My parents are sitting with family between them. They can glare at each other from opposite ends of the pew. Aunts and cousins are ready to keep them apart."

"Sounds like you got this figured out," Drake offered. "Anything else we need to know?"

"Recessional is Rodger and I first out followed by Nathan escorting our mothers. Our dads come next. Then Tina followed by Drake, Wynona, and Jon. The rest can file out behind Jon or wait until we're clear of the sanctuary." Janet had ticked each person or pairing off on her fingers. She held three fingers up, looking from Rodger to Tina back to Jon and Drake.

"Either you ran out of people or you got something else you want to tell us," Tina surmised, pointing to Janet's remaining fingers.

Janet nodded and smiled. "We definitely want this to come off smooth and easy. Some of our older relatives aren't aware of the discord and disdain happening with Rodger's parents."

Rodger cleared his throat. "I wanted to forego the reception. The minister officiating for us gave us a great suggestion."

"Dare I ask what," Jon quizzed.

Drake laughed as Janet stuck out her tongue and Rodger groaned. "Okay, I'm in, too." Drake held out his hand, palm up, toward Rodger. "Least I can do. After all you introduced us to Tina."

Rodger snickered. "That is the high point of all this, my friend. What you get to help us decide is do we party right away or wait a few hours?"

Tina threw both hands in the air, frantically waving them. "Unless you want total mayhem, you want to keep the wait minimal with your parents that close to each other."

"That's why I want a luncheon buffet immediately following so we can get them satisfied and out of our hair. Nathan and Wynona need to fly out the next morning." Janet folded her hands in her lap.

Drake stood. He yawned, placed his hands on his back, and bent backward. He straightened up and spoke. "Sounds like a solid idea to me. I'm too tired to think more."

Janet rose, yawning herself. "We're still getting used to being back ourselves. Tina, I'll call you in a couple of days."

Their good nights said, Drake followed Tina and Jon out to their cars. A few more yawns punctuated their brief discussion. Curling up together in Drake's king-size bed sounded delicious to all three. Forty minutes later, they slipped under the covers, spooned to each other with sleep claiming them shortly thereafter.

Chapter Thirty

"You know," Janet began three days later as she sat across from Tina at their favorite lunch spot, Harrigan's Café. "I wanted to ask you something the other night. It didn't feel right with the men present."

Tina sat her ice tea down. Janet could be forthright. What did she want to know?

Tina laid her hand on her lap and scrunched her napkin against her palm. Small shivers ran up and down her neck. How did she tell her best friend that some things weren't open to discussion? She wasn't sure there was much she had answers to. Honesty and respect, cornerstones of her and Janet's long-term friendship, mattered to both of them. Tina inhaled and exhaled, gathering her thoughts. Of course, she could tell Janet she didn't know the answer yet. Maybe the key was everything was open, and limitations existed based on where any of them felt the need to have them. Like Jon and Drake commented the other night as they ate dinner, polyamory's top three rules for them were respect, honesty, and continuous open communication. Some referred to it as processing. Sometimes things slowed down some. Tina called it checking in. No matter the name or label, these actions worked for them.

"Go ahead," Tina encouraged, tightening her grip on her balled-up napkin.

Janet nodded, grinning. "Bet you thought I was going to ask about sex." She paused.

Tina swallowed, wanting to respond and ask why Janet would want to know about that. Somehow teasing about sex at the moment didn't feel right. "Nah, you know how that happens between males and females."

Janet burst out laughing. "Good comeback. What I'm wondering about is arrangements. You know finding time for yourself and each of them separately."

Tina smiled, let go of her napkin, and leaned back against the booth's cushioned backrest. "We've researched how others do poly and what works in theory. For us, it's about trial and error."

"Trial and error?" Janet took a bite of her lunch.

Tina nodded. "None of us had a set schedule when we started out. Me with my crazy hours working for Frank. Drake was busy with a work project. Jon's business was ebbing and peaking inconsistently."

"Sounds like you went with the flow. Interesting way to do things. Wish Rodger and I could do that with this second ceremony." Janet wiped her mouth and drank part of her soda.

"I get that, sista." Tina ate more of her southwestern cobb salad before she spoke further. She chewed carefully, giving herself time to gather her reply and thoughts. She swallowed and spoke. "Drake and Jon don't mind taking time away from the three of us for their own time. Drake bowls every other week with a league from work. Jon spends time with his nieces and nephews once a week."

"What about time for you?" Janet forked the last of her Chicken Kiev into her mouth.

"I get it when I need it. Often one or the other has something they need to do when I feel the need for me time." Tina wiped her mouth and pushed her plate to the edge of the table.

"Sounds simple and easy. Gods, I hope this ceremony comes off as easy, too." Janet sighed and leaned on her elbow, cupping her chin.

Tina grinned. "Well the dragoness and her minions have left us alone for a bit. What do you still need to do to get you ready?"

"Pick up my dress and yours. I'm glad Torrey directed me to Mary Stockton and her shop. She did Joanna's dress and her entourage's as well." Janet emptied her soda glass. "Since we chose dresses she carried in stock, she didn't mind holding the dresses back if the others still want theirs."

"What about Wynona's dress?" Tina looked at the list Janet had laid on the table after they sat down. "Tuxedos are checked off. I know Drake owns his. Jon put his into the cleaners. It's kinda odd they own their own."

Janet nodded. "I know. Threw me, too, when Rodger said he owned one. Seems they decided when their group of friends started formal gatherings and marrying that owning one cost less than renting."

"Must be something about the class level, too." Tina combed her hands through her hair. She grimaced at the self-loathing thoughts waiting to claim her. Before, she would've given in to them. Even now a few of them still made sense. She knew better, though. Self-worth and self-esteem came from within. Jon mentioned her change as they made love last night. Tina wondered if she'd ever rid herself of these nagging feelings.

"Rodger assures me it has to do with practicality. Drake and Jon both do a lot of community fund raising and hobnobbing with the corporate elite. Black tie and formal is their normal dress code."

Tina smiled. "Drake tried his tux on the other night. Delicious and handsome. He wouldn't let me ravish him while he had his cummerbund on and his pants off."

Janet snickered. "A bit of TMI?"

Tina fanned herself and tried shaking her head no. "Jon looked scrumptious in his, too."

Janet chortled. Shaking her finger at Tina, she continued speaking. "Back to topic. Wynona got her dress done four months ago when she was in town visiting family. She's bringing hers with her."

"If the original plans could have worked out this easy, maybe you..." Tina paused, unsure if she should continue. Her opinions might not be what Janet needed or wanted to hear.

"I might not have eloped?" Janet questioned. "We might not of, but Rodger's mother is an impermeable force. As are my parents after she talked with them. There is the money, too."

"Yes, and everyone whose attending." Tina sighed as their waitress placed the bill on the table. "Everything happens for a reason. I wouldn't have met Drake and Jon if you had eloped from the beginning. Setting me up with both of them hoping for one to click with me was devious."

Janet squeezed Tina's hand. "You're a sister to me. I want the best for you. Rodger didn't tell me about their previous sharing until after we decided who to pair up for the party."

"Not that that would make a difference. Affability played a deciding factor in your and Rodger's choices I'm sure." Tina scooted to the edge of the booth seat.

"We considered personalities and common interests. Since Drake and Jon were Rodger's first choices for best man and head usher, we decided that one of them should be paired up with you." Janet picked up the check off the table and stood.

"Well, who were you pairing Nathan with?" Tina pulled two singles and a five out of her wallet. She laid them on the table. "I got the tip."

"Nathan's wife from the start. Drake and Jon both felt a relative needed to be best man since the dragoness went on about family and blood lines often." Janet made her way toward the door. Tina followed, wondering if the pageantry would come off without issue or if another episode similar to the party would break loose. She doubted any fiasco would arise. Both families would be on their best behavior. That didn't mean looks and smoldering wouldn't occur.

Ten minutes later, they exited Harrigan's and made their way up the street, walking toward Weddings and More.

Mary greeted them as they entered. "Janet and Tina, good to see you."

Mary's daughter Miriam and part-time help waved from the open doorway, allowing access to the backroom where fittings and pressings happened.

"Both of your dresses are ready. Please try them on. I want to be sure everything is correct." Mary reached for the two garment bags handing near the cash register. "Miriam will help you into the dressing rooms."

Tina walked out five minutes later. Her knee-length, A-line taffeta dress with the V-neck line fit her as if the dress were made for her from the start. Janet's choice for the accent color for the sash and band at the bottom ruffle of the skirt offset the main color without clashing. The body of the aqua dress fit her curves, accenting them in ways she hadn't thought about. The turquoise sash and ruffle enhanced the dress's flow without enveloping her or cutting her off in the middle like so many other waist-accented ones might. Tina turned around in a circle in the three-way mirror, admiring herself, wishing that Drake and Jon could see her. As she pivoted again, movement from the other dressing room caught her attention in the mirror.

Janet exited her dressing room. Her off-white, knee-length dress fit her much the same way Tina's did. The lace and beaded bodice sparkled each time light hit the beads. Mary's suggestion of replacing the spaghetti straps with wider ones made from the same material as the bodice enhanced the lace and beading more. Tina held her breath as Janet got closer. The simple, full skirt moved as Janet walked, creating an ethereal effect. Janet looked like she floated.

As Janet reached the mirror, Mary stepped up with a simple veil headpiece. Lace and beading matched that of the dress. The demi-crown of white silk, miniature roses held in place by clear hair combs capped the veil. Janet watched as Mary placed the veil on her. Both of them glanced to Tina. Shaking, Tina held her hands out to both. Tears threatened to flow. Janet and she both looked beautiful and gorgeous. Rodger along with Drake and Jon were very lucky men. Each had a woman who loved them and accepted them for themselves.

Tina squeezed Mary's hand and let go. As Tina hugged Janet, she glanced in the mirror again. Yes, life presented changes. Little had she known a year ago when she'd shared her pirate fantasy with Janet that a double treasure awaited her. Even six months prior, Jon and Drake attracted her. She didn't know how deep the chemistry and attraction went. Now she had two treasures who loved and shared her.

Janet hugged Tina and stepped away. She fanned her face close to her eyes. "I don't know why we're crying." Janet's weak smile tugged at Tina. She knew part of the feelings overwhelming her. It was like both of them entered a new phase of their life. One more thing shared together, bonding them more, bringing them closer and more like a family.

"Tears of joy?" Tina offered. "Possibly because we've found treasure. Treasure we've searched for and wished for."

Janet nodded, drying her eyes with the tissue Mary handed her. "We sure have."

A loud pop followed by a hiss sounded behind them. Miriam stood at the counter with four glasses and a bottle of carbonated white grape juice. She poured each glass half-full. "I say a toast is in order."

Mary handed a glass to Tina and one to Janet. Mary raised her glass, proposing a toast. "Here's to success in love and marriage for Janet and Rodger. And to Tina for finding her happiness and love."

The four clicked glasses together and drank. Mary promised to be at the wedding to help with last minute items as needed. Janet slid an invitation across the counter with her and Tina's checks. "Your invitation got returned by the post office. You're invited as a friend of the bride."

As Tina walked back to her car with Janet, carrying their dresses, she pondered how quickly things changed once she opened herself up to the impossible happening. Maybe time and place stayed relative to the flux in the universe once she acknowledged her need and desire. Challenges remained along with learning and growing. No longer alone, she knew she could and would be all right.

Epilogue

Two weeks later

Tina stood at the front of the church next to Wynona. Her dress complimented Tina's with slight differences. The sash and last ruffle on the skirt were aqua while the main portions of the dress were turquoise. Wynona's dark hair and olive-toned complexion glowed against the color. Her smile reached her eyes and curled her lips. Tina felt her own smile grow as Wynona's fiancé Ricardo blew her an airborne kiss. The man was a romantic for sure. He'd gone down on one knee before the other guests began arriving and proposed. The quarter-carat emerald surrounded by ruby chips glittered under the spot lights near the pulpit. The gold setting looked lovely on Wynona's long fingers and manicured nails.

Tina glanced down to her own hands. A ring bejeweled each of her ring fingers, promise gifts from Jon and Drake. Three circles intertwined from Jon graced her left hand. On her right, a small heart encircled with each of their birth stones, a gift from Drake. Around her neck, as well as Wynona's, hung Janet's bridal gift to each of them. A twenty-four carat gold chain with their initials hanging from them adorned their necks.

Beethoven's "Ode to Joy" sounded. Everyone stood as the doors to the narthex opened. Janet came down the aisle, beaming. She stopped at her parents' pew, hugging them. Rodger made his way down to her, first shaking hands with his father who sat two pews behind and on the opposite end from his soon-to-be ex. Before Rodger offered Janet his arm, he embraced his mother. They spoke briefly. He kissed her cheek after shaking his head no. He turned, offered Janet his arm, and moved forward until they stood in front of the minister.

As Rodger and Janet exchanged their vows for the second time, Tina glanced out at the guests present. Joanna and Stuart accompanied by Holt and Torrey sat amongst the relatives keeping peace between Rodger's parents who glared at each other from time to time. Stuart's Grandma Getty sat with Rodger's Aunt Esmeralda, who nudged Mrs. Daniels every time she snuck a peek at her unwanted spouse. Tina nibbled her lip to keep from laughing. She looked to where Janet's friends and family sat. Mary and Miriam sat close to Janet's second cousin Ross. Chatter down at Frank's was Ross and Mary might be dating.

Drake and Jon blew Tina kisses as Celine Dion's "Because You Loved Me" began. Janet and Rodger proceeded down the aisle and out of the sanctuary. Nathan followed as planned with both mothers on his arm. Tina took her place behind the fathers and filed out. Wynona, Drake, and Jon followed as rehearsed and planned. At the back of the sanctuary, Rodger and Janet re-entered, inviting everyone to join them in the fellowship hall for lunch and refreshments.

As the afternoon passed, Tina made her way around the room, mingling with everyone present. Each time she got near Drake and Jon, they paused, touched her hand or arm, and smiled. Around four-thirty, chairs and tables began moving to one side of the room. One table held music equipment with CDs and tapes. Nathan shook hands with the DJ, taking the microphone to the sound system from him.

"Testing," Nathan said. A bit of reverb echoed through the hall. "Okay, now that I have your attention, let's get this party started. First, the tossing of the garter. Then the bouquet."

Cheers and applause broke out. Janet sat on a chair in the middle of the open space. Rodger knelt down making a big show of working the white and blue garter down her leg. He kissed it, spun in a circle and tossed. Laughter broke out. The garter landed on top of Ross's head. He plucked it off and re-tossed it. Several tosses later, Drake snatched the garter out of the air and declared it rightfully belonged to Ross who, red-faced and smiling, accepted the garter. He stuffed it in his suit coat pocket.

Janet kicked off her shoes and stood on the chair she'd been sitting on. With her back to the group of women surrounding her, she tossed her bouquet over her shoulder. Tina backed up as several women rushed toward the back of the room. She kept backing up until she backed into Drake and Jon, who held her loosely against them. Someone yelled, "Heads up!"

Tina looked up. Coming down at her was the bouquet. She reached up and caught it. Warm laughter rushed over her shoulders. She looked at Drake and Jon. Both grinned back at her. Jon spoke first. "Looks like we're next."

"Yes, it does," Drake confirmed.

Tina's eyes closed as both men kissed her cheek. Her heart pounded yes, they were next. Her happy ending was just beginning.

THE END

Don't miss out!

Visit the website below and you can sign up to receive emails whenever Solara Gordon publishes a new book. There's no charge and no obligation.

https://books2read.com/r/B-A-RAUJ-WGQKC

BOOKS 2 READ

Connecting independent readers to independent writers.

Did you love *Three Hearts In Love*? Then you should read *Love's Triple Play*[1] by Solara Gordon!

[2]

Jeff Nickerson believes his personal relationship with his business partner Mary Bates is strong and ready to grow now that he's back in Cascade Bay. Mary is dating her other business partner Ron Bailey who she has a lot in common with. Ron's looking for a primary relationship and he's certain Mary's the one.

Mary still cares for Jeff along with her growing affection for Ron. Ron's ready to share Mary with Jeff, their silent business partner. First Ron must educate Mary and Jeff about polyamory and shared relationships.

Can three business partners grow into three in love when they mix love, sex, and work? Will uncertainty and moving outside their individual comfort zones stop them from trying?

Read more at https://solaragordon.com/.

1. https://books2read.com/u/mY6Myd

2. https://books2read.com/u/mY6Myd

Also by Solara Gordon

Watch for more at https://solaragordon.com/.

About the Author

Solara loves and lives with her partner of 21 years in the Metro DC area. What started out as a bi-coastal romance soon settled on one coast.

A vivid imagination keeps her busy creating her next fascinating romance. She enjoys creating unique characters and watching their journeys unfold. "Love freely given multiplies and will return endlessly" is a key aspect of her stories. Add in alternative lifestyles and her love for the paranormal, and the uncommon becomes the norm in many of her stories.

Her day job in the financial services industry pays the bills while she pens her erotic tales.

Read more at https://solaragordon.com/.